The

Mysteries of Verbena House;

OR,

MISS BELLASIS

BIRCHED FOR THIEVING.

BY ETONENSIS

BIRCHGROVE PRESS

http://www.birchgrovepress.com

ISBN:
978-0-9870956-0-2

The Mysteries of Verbena House; or, Miss Bellasis Birched for Thieving was first published as two volumes in one in 1882. Only 150 copies were issued, probably by William Lazenby, at the price of four guineas. The first volume was issued in 1881 under the half-title: *Birched for Thieving, or the Punishment of Miss Bellasis*. The second volume and the full title appeared in 1882. The authorship is uncertain: 'Etonensis' is a pseudonym. It signifies an old Etonian, that is, someone who has been to Eton College. Volume one is usually attributed to the popular Victorian journalist George Augustus Sala. James Campbell Reddie, an author and collector of erotica, is often credited as the author of volume two. Edited by Mark McDougal for Birchgrove Press.

CONTENTS

The

Mysteries of Verbena House

TOME I

BIRCHED FOR THIEVING,

OR

THE PUNISHMENT OF MISS BELLASIS.

Verbena House, Sussex-square, Kemp Town, Brighton, was the most fashionable, the most expensive, and the best conducted of the ladies' schools with which the Queen of Watering-places abounds. It did not profess to be either a "seminary," "college," or an "institute."

Miss Sinclair, its proprietess, always spoke of her establishment as a "school," and of herself as a "schoolmistress." Nay, she even went so far, sometimes, as to call her scholars her "girls." To her servants, of course, they were the "young ladies;" to the assistant governesses they were "the pupils;" but to Miss Sinclair they were simply "girls," and as such she treated them.

She had no less than fifty disciples under her charge, ranging, in age, between eight and sixteen. She had a firmly established maximum and minimum as to years, and seldom departed from it.

"Under eight," she was accustomed to say, "a girl's a baby, and is fitter for a nursery than a school, over sixteen she's a woman, and as likely as not to run away with a captain of hussars, or the French master, or the baker's man."

Miss Sinclair even, in view of the susceptibilities of the more precocious of her girls between fourteen and sixteen, looked very sharply after all subalterns of horse, all teachers of French, and all bearers of bread baskets. One never knew what might happen.

She was a fine, tall, shapely "maid-matron"—if you will accept the paradox—of about two-and-thirty.

I mean that although she was "Miss Sinclair" to all outward intents and purposes, and not a whisper had ever been uttered against her fair fame, her form was yet so richly and voluptuously developed, her eyes were so full of light, and her lips of colour, that it seemed a misuse of terms to speak of her as a spinster. Those eyes, by the way, were hazel. She had very small, white, plump, and yet firm-looking hands. Her hair was of a "dove-coloured" brown, and she wore it in smooth bandeaux beneath a cap, about the size of a modern bonnet, of richt point lace. She dressed, usually, in black watered silk, with a gold chain round her neck, terminating with a dainty watch and trinkets at her waist and worn outside the belt, the massiveness of which chain many an alderman might have envied.

All that was known of Miss Sinclair was that she had been governess in the family of the Marchioness of Courdesart—now Duchess of Tadmor, you will remember—and that she had successfully educated her ladyship's four daughters, the beautious Ladies Palmyra, Tyra, Sidonia, and Ephesia Wildernesse. On the marriage of the last-named with Lord Baalbee, Miss Sinclair retired from the service of the noble house of Courdesart, now Tadmor.

The testimonials with which she was favoured by her distinguished patroness were of the most flattering description; and to these, it may be conjectured, a reward of a more substantial nature was added, since, shortly after the departure of Miss Sinclair from Wildernesse House, Park-lane, London, she commenced the career of schoolmistress in Sussex-square, Brighton.

Verbena House was an immense mansion, which had formerly been the residence of a railway contractor who made a million of money, but, suddenly smashing, paid his creditors a dividend of one penny three farthings in the pound, and has since, poor fellow, been compelled to live in comparative obscurity in Eaton-place, Belgravia, his wife having under her settlement not more than six or seven thousand a year.

The palace of this commercial Belisarius had, with ease been transformed into a school. The enormous bedrooms were divided and sub-divided by neatly painted and varnished bulk heads into compartments, each of which contained a bed. As many as ten could sleep in one room, but each pupil had her separate couch, and was strictly isolated from her companions.

Miss Sinclair was of opinion that although self-abuse had been termed the "solitary vice," girls are very often led, in the first instance, to frig themselves through the evil example of some bedfellow who has already graduated in depravity. "Evil communications corrupt good manners," held Miss Sinclair, and so she made her girls sleep alone.

Whenever a pupil thus isolated was detected, or convicted after suspicion, in frigging herself, she was, in the first instance, handed over to the care of the medical man-in-ordinary, Dr. Jossup.

This practitioner administered to her a course of medicines, mainly of a strongly purgative nature. Her bed was moved to one of the governess's rooms, or, in extreme cases, to Miss Sinclair's. She was treated with extreme kindness; her schoolfellows were merely informed that she was "delicate", and required "great care", and the servants were strictly prohibited from saying anything about her real ailment, even when, as very rarely happened, they knew anything about it. Not under any circumstances was the poor sufferer punished for that which is more a foible than a fault. Powdered camphor was strewn, according to Raspail's system, between the sheets and the blankets of her bed, and small muslin bags containing the same substance were sewn on either side of the anterior slit of her drawers. Camphor, as is well-known, is a very powerful sedative. Of the abominable French invention called "caleçon préventif" and which consists of a pair of washleather breeches with only a small circular orifice between the thighs for mincturation, and belted, buckled and padlocked round the waist, precisely like the old Cadenas with which the Crusaders locked up their wives' quims when they went to the Holy Land, Miss Sinclair would not hear.

Admiral Bowley, whose daughter, aged thirteen, was continually discounting the delights of the nuptial bed, sent such a pair of culottes, with his compliments, to Miss Sinclair, for his daughter's use, but the schoolmistress indignantly returned them. The apparatus had been recommended to him by the French lady with whom he was accustomed to fornicate, and occasionally to indulge in pederasatism in Paris.

Poor Josephine! I knew her well. She died of inflammation of the vagina, owing to the breaking of the string attached to the sponge with which she always took care to plug her cunt before she was fucked.

But this is a digression. Miss Sinclair would have none of the admiral's washleather breeches, so he took his daughter away from school in a huff. He subsequently told his attached personal friend, Colonel Sloofly, late of the Second Life Guards, at the Senior United Service, that by the grace of God, and a stout cat-o'-nine-tails—"three knots in each tail my boy"—he had "cured the young jade of making a beast of herself."

"Cat-o'-nine-tails," quoth Sloofly, his eyes twinkling, he was a notorious old lecher, "of course you gave it her over her clothes."

The admiral was a widower. "Of course," he replied, "I did nothing of the sort. I gave it her upon her bare arse, and my housekeeper held her head between her legs whilst I lashed her. I gave her four dozen in one day, and I think that sickened her. If I'd thought of it I'd have sent for you, Sloofly."

Miss Clara Bowley is now married to the Reverend Septimus Twigg, Rector of Badsworth, Leicestershire. She takes much interest in her husband's schools; and, in the boys' department, at least, has succeeded in persuading her husband in substituting the rod for the cane, which last she inveighs against as abominably cruel as an implement of chastisement. She has already caused several little urchins to be horsed and birched, although to her infinite disappointment her husband would not permit her to be present at the infliction of the punishment.

"The spectacle," he observed, "was one calculated to

wound equally her feelings of delicacy and of humanity."

Nor has she yet been successful in obtaining the Reverend Septimus's consent to her often-urged proposal that the girls as well as the boys should be birched. The reverend is a soft-hearted, and, withal, a modest man.

"A few stripes on their hands or shoulders, my dear Clara, if you like," he replied, "but surely you would not destroy the earliest grains of modesty in the female mind, by subjecting a girl-child to a punishment at once indecent and degrading."

"I've been flogged myself, over and over again," pouts Mrs. Rector.

"More shame to the brute who dared to lay a hand on my Clara," adds her husband, who is decidedly a Benedict of the "spooney" order.

"I should like you a great deal better if you flogged me," thinks Clara. The knots of the old admiral's cat-o'-nine-tails yet tingle on her rump, and set her thoughts on fire. In destroying one devil of lubricity her father had only awakened another. I fancy that Mrs. Clara will have her way some day, and initiate her lord into the mysteries of flagellation. Probably many a village school girl's posterior will be sacrificed on the altar of their mutual loves.

Another digression; but I disdain to apologise for it. This narrative will be made up, more or less, of digressions and divergences.

For the nonce, however, I return to Miss Sinclair's method of curing masturbation in her pupils. She was quite as much opposed to the use of horse-hair gloves—a common corrective in such cases—as to that of the famous "caleçon préventif." "Masturbation," thus she dogmatised, "arises from morbid imagination, combined with local irritation, producing titillation,

15

and that is not to be cured by excoriation. If a girl is really bent on abusing herself, she would do it were her hands covered with thorns and fish-hooks."

Miss Sinclair was right. Her system, however, had its limits.

If Dr. Jossop's purgatives the camphored sheets and camphored drawers, did not succeed, the victim of Onanism was quietly sent away from the school. She was not expelled, her parents were mildly but firmly bidden to remove her. Miss Sinclair never divulged the secret; and it was the interest of the sufferer's friends to be equally reticent. La vie ne se passe pas d'immenses ensevelissements.

There were fifty pupils then, many of them daughters of noblemen or baronets, none of a lower grade than children of rich country gentlemen, officers in the army or navy, or beneficed clergymen.

Miss Sinclair's term for a "little one" were never under one hundred guineas a year; for a girl above fourteen she often wanted two hundred.

At the period to which this narrative refers the school contained perhaps thirty girls of the junior category; that is to say children wearing petticoats short enough to display some portion of their drawers; and twenty elder pupils, wearing long skirts, and whose "pantalettes" were consequently only visible to the eye of the profane vulgar when they were walking on the Marine Parade, and when the wind blew very high. But that every one of her girls, little and big, should wear drawers of some kind or another was part of Miss Sinclair's code of laws, and those laws were as those of the Medes and Persians. Thus there were little minxes whose breeches only reached to the knee, and others whose trousers only came mid-leg, and a few who wore the old fashioned drawers, which came down to the ankle, and well nigh covered the boot. Some of the elder girls wore drawers almost as tight as nun's pantaloons, and whole seated—that is to say not slit up the back. These buttoned at the sides, and necessitated the letting down of a hinder flap when the wearer went to the watercloset. Others, again, patronised "knickerbocker" drawers of crimson or purple flannel—Zouave breeches in fact, secured by an "elastic" at the knee—but the majority of the elder girls wore the ordinary undergarments of English ladies, young and old, linen or longcloth "tongs," slit up the front and the back, tying round the waist with a string, the drawers themselves reaching to the middle of the calf of the leg, and decorated at the extremities with several "tucks," or with embroidery or "insertion."

One girl, Miss Montes, from Cuba, a "big one," wore regular Turkish drawers of transparent gauze, which bagged down to her ankles. She had brought three dozen pairs of these curious inexpressibles with her from Havana. "They were useful," she said, "in the Tropics, as a protection against mosquitoes."

Miss Sinclair kept a splendid table for her pupils. The girls had wine, or beer, or water with their meals precisely as their parents chose; but no increase or diminution of charge was made by the school mistress in consequence.

They had four meals regularly every day—breakfast, dinner, tea, and supper; and in case of intermediate hunger bread and jam or plum cake were always procurable.

The studies were varied and numerous, and the young ladies were certainly neither encouraged or suffered to be idle; but the hours of recreation were sufficient, and bathing and outdoor exercise formed no inconsiderable part of them. Wednesdays and Saturdays were half-holidays.

There were four resident governesses: Miss Everard,

head English teacher, and "first lieutenant," so to speak, to Admiral Sinclair, K.C.B. Miss E. was forty-one, thin, hard, angular, cross, cantankerous, but conscientious. The girls feared but respected her.

Next in the gubernational hierarchy came Mademoiselle De la Tourelle, French teacher; a little yellow woman, with frizzy black hair, and eyes that twinkled like beads. The girls made fun of her; she was passionate but very good-hearted, and seldom reported them for misconduct.

Third came Fraulein Schrobbs, German and music teacher—at least in the latter capacity she superintended the "practice" of the younger girls, and prepared the advanced ones for the lessons of the professors. She was a sour, listless, placid, pudding-faced woman, going through her drudgery in a sufficing but apathetic manner; yawning fearfully when it was over, and occasionally given to whimpering in secret about Vaterland. She was adored by the girls because she was sentimental, and talked to them about Charlotte and Werter, and sometimes sang Schubert's dreamy and dreary songs to them.

Fourth and last came Miss Cope, junior English teacher, superintendent of order in the playground and at the promenade, directress of the bathing machine's, and general spy, tale-teller, and fetcher and carrier. She was cordially hated by the entire establishment, including her fellow-teachers and the domestics; while Miss Sinclair, though she found Miss Cope useful, heartily despised her. She had been recommended by the mama of a rich pupil, and had come, it was rumoured, from some orphan school. The big girls were apt to whisper maliciously among themselves that Miss Cope had received her education in a reformatory.

Six servants were kept in this luxuriously-appointed

boarding-school—a cook, three housemaids and a scullery maid; a boy who cleaned the knives and did odd jobs, including a few not contemplated by his mistress, such as fetching in pastry and sweet-stuff for the young ladies, and conveying their clandestine correspondence to and from the post office and finally, a house-keeper, who had charge of the wardrobe, gave out the clean linen, carved at table, and remained in the bathroom on "sloushing" nights to see that no unseemly gambols took place, particularly when the fair bathers were having their limbs dried by the housemaids.

It is scarcely necessary to mention the different professors who attended to give lessons at Verbena House, and, indeed, at present, to enumerate these accomplished gentlemen after cooks and housemaids is to subject them to some indignity.

Craving their pardon, in any case, I will just put on record the fact that Herr Shrumpff, from Leipzig, gave lessons on the pianoforte; that Signor Caldemonte taught singing; that Monsieur Beauvallet gave lessons in French literature; that Mr.Sparigall was the dancing, and Mr. Mc Guilp the drawing masters; and that Sergeant-Major Home, formerly of the Blues, imparted instruction in callisthenics and the use of the Indian scepter.

Special masters also attended when required for the Italian language, and for botany and geology.

The spiritual director and father, confessor of this interesting nursery was the Rev. Arthur Philip Calvedon, of St. Aidan's Chapel, St. James's-street, an ecclesiastic of high ritualistic tendencies, and a very handsome and engaging gentleman, about thirty years old, to boot.

The medical man, as I have previously stated, was Dr. Jossop, of the Old Steyne.

There remains only one subject to be mentioned to complete this scholastic microcosm.

What, it may be asked, was the scheme of discipline pursued at Verbena House? Of what nature were the rewards and punishments? How did Miss Sinclair contrive to manage fifty girls, of whom twenty were between the difficult ages or fourteen and sixteen?

Among the fifty there were demons and there were clever idlers. There were unruly spirits, and there were tomboys and hoyden. Many were slovenly and two or three positively dirty in their habits.

Miss Waterhouse habitually pea'd the bed.

Miss Clayton's drawers were always in a sad state, owing to her forgetting to take paper with her when she went to the watercloset.

Miss Moleskin was continually in trouble for neglecting to wash her ears and under her arms.

Then there were girls who were gluttons, and girls who were liars.

Miss Gallick was always fighting; Miss Blandford was a practical joker, the principal victims of her jokes being the governesses; Miss Mornington was a "sleepy head"; and Miss Landor a "crybaby."

Some of the fifty were really good, quite studious, affectionate girls, doing and thinking no harm; but the best of girls will be naughty, if not troublesome, sometimes, and require reproof or punishment.

Of reproof there was always enough and to spare at Verbena House.

The four governesses had the privilege of scolding their pupils, and carried it out to the fullest extent.

Miss Everard "nagged"; Mademoiselle de la Tourelle scolded; Fraulein Schrobbs bleated forth reprimands in a lachrymose tone; and Miss Cope searled vindictive threats of "reporting" everybody to Miss Sinclair. She never failed to keep her promise. And Miss Sinclair—

well, she could scold as well as her subordinates but she could also punish.

But how? Pray don't jump at a hasty conclusion. Pray do not incontinently assume that Miss Sinclair's sovereign remedies for the ills to which her school was heir, were the birch, the cane, the strap, the horsewhip, or the knotted whipcord.

All such implements of flagellation I have known to be used in ladies' schools; to say nothing of the whalebone busk of a pair of stays, a hair brush, a skipping rope, a bamboo, a bed cord, a bunch of nettles—they sting frightfully, without making any noise—a ruler, and the open hand.

Nay, I have heard of one governess who flogged, or rather "birched" a girl's bottom with a wet towel, twisted so as to form at both ends a sharp point. Let me hasten to assure you that Miss Sinclair was not by any means a flogging schoolmistress, and that up to the time of the drama I am about to relate had never seen such a thing as a birch rod. She had heard of it, of course, vaguely as a bunch of twigs with which children were scourged, but she had neither felt it in her own childhood, nor used it on any of her pupils.

Of course she had an instinctive idea of what "whipping" and "flogging" meant, and that the bare bottom was the proper place for such exercitation. She even drew a subtle distinction between the synonyms, and tacitly assumed that boys were "flogged," and girls "whipped." The former seemed the rougher and severer form.

While governess at Wildernesse House she had never been permitted to lay a finger on her pupils. When they misbehaved complaint was made to their parents, and according to the ladies' maid it was no uncommon occurrence for Lord Courdesart, when he came home to dinner to send for one of his daughters into his library, and horsewhip her soundly.

Lady Palmyra was so horsewhipped, the maid said, when she was nearly eighteen years of age but my lord refrained from putting up his daughter's clothes. He did not even make her bare her shoulders, but lashed her over the back over her dress. The truth was his lordship was a brute, and not an artist.

Who but a brute would wheal a poor girl's back and shoulders with a heavy horsewhip? A delicate, cutting, whistling switch applied to the bare backside gives exquisite pleasure to the performer, and while (of course) it lasts, does not disfigure the patient.

I don't say that although Miss Sinclair had been hitherto a stranger to the birch both in an active and passive sense, that she had wholly abstained from corporal punishment in the government of her school. Nay, on several occasions during her three years' occupancy of Verbena House she had manipulated the bare bum of a refractory pupil, and administered a sound, but alas, a sadly unscientific whipping.

There was Miss Gallick, for example, the pugilistic girl. Coming into the French schoolroom one morning Miss Sinclair found Miss Landor, aged twelve, the "crybaby," blubbering most piteously. The ferocious Gallick had absolutely given her school-fellow a black eye.

Losing all patience at this aggravated assault the schoolmistress caught the assailant a couple of smart boxes on the ears.

Would you believe it that Miss Gallick had the hardihood to kick her Mistress's shins.

Now, fairly enraged, Miss Sinclair seized the young gladiator and dragged her up stairs to her bedroom, locked the door, flung her on the bed, threw her clothes over her head, and began to "lay on to her posterior" with her open hand. She struck the girl as hard as she could, and with repeated blow, but they did not seem to make the slightest impression on Miss Gallick.

The schoolmistress had been in such an extreme hurry to execute justice that she had forgotten to pull down the offender's drawers. This oversight she proceeded to remedy; but Miss Gallick's breeches were tied under her stays and chemise, and Miss Sinclair was compelled to drag them down by main force, breaking the string.

She now proceeded with her "spanking" on the bare cheeks of the girl's arse, leaving her finger marks impressed in bright crimson on the flesh; but she could not avoid the impression that she was hurting her hand much more than she was hurting Miss Gallick's bottom.

Indeed, the pugilist turned round, with an impudent air, and said that "she did not care."

"I'll make you care, my lady," said Miss Sinclair; "I'll make you holloa, if I stand over you all day."

She looked round for some more formidable weapon of chastisement, and her eye lighted on a slipper with a somewhat stout sole, perfectly smooth. Seizing this, and passing her left hand round the girl's loins; she went to work with a will, and the crimson finger marks were soon obliterated beneath the more portentous stigmata of the slipper.

With the last-named Miss Gallick must have received at least fifty sound thwacks, laid on with the utmost forte of the muscular arm of her corrector; and, although her backside did not assume what is known among flagellants as the "plum pudding" aspect, that is, when the bottom is covered with dark curious bumps and bars, from some of which the blood slowly oozes, enough execution had been done to make the hemispheres of Miss Gallick's rump one *field gules*, which took a few hours afterwards a livid hue. Her bottom was in fact black and blue for a fortnight.

She profited considerably by the chastisement, and did not offer to fight any one for a very long time; but still the reader, will, I think, be inclined to agree with me that her correction was more of the nature of a "beating" than a flogging or whipping. She was thrashed rather than flagellated.

One again had Miss Sinclair operated with some severely on the back settlements of one of her scholars. This was in the case of Miss Clayton, aged twelve, the careless young lady who would not take paper with her to the w.c., and so soiled her white longcloth breeches. She had committed this nasty offence so often that the schoolmistress determined to "make an example of her."

On the report of the housekeeper, Mrs. Rumble, that the young lady's drawers were again in an unseemly condition, she was ordered down to the scullery, and the housekeeper standing over her with instructions to slap her across the shoulders if she was refractory, she was made to soap, scrub, and wash out the offending garments in a tub of hot water.

Having wrung the drawers well out, she was made to stretch them over a clothes line, and in about an hour afterwards Miss Sinclair came down to the kitchen—a very rare occurrence with her—and lectured Miss Clayton severely on her uncleanly habits.

She was about to dismiss her without further punishment to her own room, when a piece of the clothes line lying loose on the scullery table seemed to strike her. She took it in her hand, and measuring it, found that it would double into four lengths, about a foot-and-a-half long. She tied three lengths in a knot, at one extremity, and a very satisfactory cat-of-eights tails was thus formed. The clothes line was about as thick as the holder of a magnum bonum pen.

"Come here, you dirty hussey," cried Miss Sinclair, swaying this scourge to and fro.

Miss Clayton approached, whimpering.

"Hold out your hand," Swash! swash! swash! (not "swish," mind), "Now the other."

The girl's palms were held out in succession. She draws them backwards and forwards quickly, wincing under each cut, her shoulders nervously twitching, but beyond a murmured "oh dear!" she uttered no exclamation.

"I'll whip you," said Miss Sinclair, suddenly. "Mrs. Rumble, pull her petticoats up."

The house-keeper, nothing loath, for the dirty little minx was not a favourite, obeyed, and threw Miss Clayton's clothes above her head.

Although she had just washed one pair of breeches she had another pair on, for the garments on which the unfavourable report had been made belonged to the previous day. They were drawers of the kind I described as "whole seated," buttoning at the sides, and coming down in flaps.

"Pull down her drawers," quoth Miss Sinclair, "and hold her across your lap, Mrs. Rumble."

The house-keeper followed these directions, first seating herself in a kitchen chair, and Miss Clayton's arse, a ridiculously fat one, by the way, was exposed to view, her drawers hanging about her legs. Mrs. Rumble kept tight hold of her round the waist with one arm; the other she placed across her thighs, grasping her just above the knee, while, for additional security, she raised one of her own stout legs, and with it fast locked both Miss Clayton's ankles. The girl was as helpless as though she had been in a vice.

"I served her as I used to when my 'usband used to whack one of the young 'uns," Mrs. Rumble subsequently explained to Mrs. Cleaver, the cook.

"Good Lord, how he used to pay my Polly with a 'unting whip when she was almost a woman grown, for gallivanting after the fellows. But he didn't forget to gallivant with me after he'd done welting her. Ah! poor dear! poor dear!"

Thus Mrs. Rumble, whom I left tightly holding the dirty Miss Clayton across her lap, as a shower of stripes from the four times doubled clothes line quickly descended on her plump white bottom, thought.

The cord happened to be damp almost to wetness, and the consequence was that each stripe raised a sharp wheal. Miss Clayton's arse speedily assumed the appearance of a gridiroe.

"You'd better cross the cuts, ma'am," observed Mrs. Rumble, in a low tone to Miss Sinclair, when the girl had received about a dozen stripes and a half, each one eliciting a shriek from her.

"What do you mean, Rumble?" asked Miss Sinclair, pausing in her task.

"Hit her cross ways, instead of straight towards you; that'll let the bruised blood out, ma'am. If you don't she'll be badly cut, and, perhaps, it'll fester."

Following this advice, the schoolmistress shifted her position, and let the scourge fall right across Clayton's rump, instead of vertically from the small of her back towards her cunt. A charming "cross-cut" pattern of wheals was thus produced, and at the intersection of the lines the blood, released from extravastation, to flow.

How long this might have continued it is uncertain; but the punishment was brought to sudden termination by the indelicate behaviour of Miss

Clayton, who appeared to be of a leaky nature both forward and astern, and who pea'd all over Mrs. Rumble's wet apron, and by certain unmistakable symptoms in an opposite direction, gave warning that she was about still farther to relieve nature, and in a manner even still more indecorous.

"The nasty, dirty, filthy, wretch," said the disgusted schoolmistress, gathering all her strength into one farewell cut of peculiar poignancy, "there, take her away, Mrs. Rumble, and give her a bath, and flog her again, if you like. I'll have nothing more to do with the nasty little beast."

Mrs. Rumble observed deferentially "that it was not for the likes of her to whip a young lady's backside," yet nevertheless, when she had given Miss Clayton a warm bath, and dried her thoroughly with a rough huckaback towel—the application of which made the nymph of the bruised bottom squeal prodigiously—the housekeeper was tempted to use the power with which she was invested by the principal of Verbena House, and throwing the newly-washed girl, stark naked as she was, across her knee, she administered to her a round dozen of cuts with the flesh brush.

Clayton howled dismally, and threatened to write to her papa, who was a Yorkshire baronet.

Upon this the flesh brush went to work again; whereupon Clayton begged for mercy, and being released from Mrs. Rumble's knee, huddled on her drawers, and, let me add, never dirtied them again.

The alacrity with which, on all subsequent occasions, she provided herself with soft paper before resorting to "Naboth's vineyard" was as surprising as it was edifying.

These were really the only two severe cases of corporal punishment which had occurred in Miss Sinclair's establishment since her ascension to scholastic office; and, in neither case, as has been seen, was chastisement inflicted in a deliberate, solemn, and scholastic manner. With Miss Gallick, as with Miss Clayton, the schoolmistress had only acted on the spur of the moment, and in the heat of passion; yet both punishments had effected their purpose, and proved a most salutary correction to the pupils.

Enough has been said, however, to show that Miss Sinclair could not hitherto lay claim to the character of a "flogging schoolmistress," and I very much doubt whether such "flogging schoolmistresses" do really exist, save in some rare and occult instances, where ci-devant gay women are set up in business by wealthy flagellants for the express purpose of carrying on the birch discipline—the performances being witnessed by the amateurs through crevices or peep holes in doors, or from behind curtains, or from some other secure point of espial. Ceci est un livre de bonne foy, lecteur, as old Montaigne says.

I am not narrating fiction, but fact; and throughout the entire story of Miss Bellasis I shall have but very rarely to draw on my imagination. On the other hand I would point out that the vast majority of stories of systematic birching in girls' schools which appear in the correspondence columns of newspapers and periodicals are gross fables, invented either to tickle the fancy of the writers who write them, or cunningly devised as decoy-ducks to draw forth genuine communications from correspondents writing in good faith.

Such, I am certain, were three-fourths of the whipping queries and answers inserted in recent numbers of the "Englishwoman's Domestic Magazine."

While entering this caveat I would not have you suppose that girls are never flogged at school. They are, and that soundly and frequently, and on their bottoms too.

The study of the phenomena of flagellation has been the business of my life, and I have scarcely ever conversed with a woman in any rank of life, from the highest to the lowest, from whom I have not succeeded in eventually drawing the avowal that at some period of her life she had been whipped or flogged in an indecent manner, either by her parents or at school.

There are very few schoolmistresses also who do not occasionally resort to flogging, and many are very fond of the exercise; but they generally keep their executions a profound secret, and certainly would not blurt out their experiences in the columns of a newspaper.

A bed-room, with the door well locked, is usually the scene of these Eleusinian mysteries, and the sufferer keeps the secret as closely as the executioner does.

When schoolmistresses flog I believe that they use a cane, a whip—probably a gutta percha one—a strap, or a cord, much oftener than they do the birch; for the simple reason that birch rods are very difficult of procurement, and that governesses are ashamed to send out their servants in quest of such articles.

Thus, I think, nothing has been extenuated, and nothing set down in malice respecting the discipline of Miss Sinclair's school. That lady could flog, and had flogged on occasions, as nine-tenths of the scholastic sisterhood have done; but she made no unnecessary parade of being a flogster, and had any inquisitive commissioner of middle-class education forwarded her a form to fill up, she would probably have left in blank the space headed, "What punishments do you make use of?" or else inserted the discreet answer, "Such as I deem suited to the offence."

At Verbena House, then, not only was the birch absent, but not so much as cane was kept in the house.

There was no "whipping-room," no "horse," and no "block."

Now and again a cautious mamma, before placing her daughter with Miss Sinclair, would ask, "Pray, Madam, is there any whipping in your school?"

To which the schoolmistress would deliver a stereotyped reply, "I hope no young lady in my school would ever do anything to deserve whipping; but if she did I should most assuredly seek counsel of her parents before resorting to extreme measures."

The majority of mammas would be quite satisfied with this; but to a few, who pushed the question home, Miss Sinclair would say, "May I ask if you disapprove of corporal punishment under any circumstances?"

If the mamma said "Yes," Miss Sinclair hastened to assure her that so long as her daughter remained at Verbena House not a finger should be laid upon her; and this promise, once made, Miss Sinclair would most scrupulously keep.

It would occasionally happen, however, that a parent frankly admitted that her daughter was very difficult to manage, and that a good whipping now and then would do her good.

To such an admission the schoolmistress had likewise a conventional answer, "We shall see, my dear Madam; we shall see, and act for the best."

Miss Gallick, the pugilist, and Miss Clayton, the "smear-tail," had been among the young ladies to whom, in their mammas' opinion, an occasional whipping would do no harm; and Miss Sinclair had not failed to profit by the hint given her.

With the elder girls, however, I mean those in "long dresses," between fourteen and sixteen, she had never gone beyond a box on the ears, or a smart smack across the bare shoulders.

Stay; I am wrong.

Several of the young ladies took horse exercise, and Miss Sinclair, who was a splendid equestrienne, always accompanied them, for those Brighton riding-masters, my dear, have a very sad reputation for "gallivanting."

One day she told Miss Talbot, a slim, fair-haired, beauty, full sixteen years old, and extremely obstinate and wilful, that she intended to take a canter on the cliff, and instructed her to go up stairs and dress.

It was about eleven in the morning. The horses had been sent for from Wigdon's livery stable, and were waiting at the door.

Miss Sinclair's equestrian toilet was soon completed; and very stately and comely indeed did she look in dark-blue riding habit, with a neatly-varnished boot peeping from beneath her skirt, and a cavalier hat with a sweeping scarlet feather.

She wore riding trousers, of course, "chamois leather with black feet," as the advertisements have it, the leather portion reaching from the waist to the top of the thigh.

I don't know how it is, but to me there is something exceedingly randy in the notion of a modest woman putting on riding trousers. Her drawers she slips on and off without much troubling herself about them. They are slit before and behind, and when she has occasion to sit down, or to squat they open of themselves; and, indeed, in undressing, I have often seen a woman divest herself of drawers and petticoats with one unloosing movement.

But riding trousers cannot be treated in this unceremonious manner. The wearer must be measured for them—a randy proceeding to begin with. They may be measured by a woman; but the artisans who make the breeches are men—randy preceding number two.

Then they must be tried on, well fitted between the fork, well smoothed over the buttocks, well trained down the calves of the legs; and, finally, they must be worn.

The greatest enemy to a woman's chastity is contact. Let her wear her things loose, and she may keep her blood cool. Nuns—continental ones at, least—don't wear drawers. Peasant women, who are chaste enough as times go, don't wear drawers; and when they stoop you may see the bare flesh of their thighs above their ungartered stockings. But the bigger the whore—professional or otherwise—the nicer will be the drawers she wears, while the prude, or the cantankerous old maid will either wear the most hideous breeches imaginable, or none at all. I positively knew a lady once who not only repudiated drawers herself, but would not allow her daughters to wear them.

"They were immodest," she said. And so they are. They bring into immediate contact with a woman something belonging to the opposite sex.

When drawers are made of linen, and are bifurcated at the bottom and belly, they are feminised to an extent which may neutralise the elements I have spoken of; although, as far as I am concerned, it tickles me somewhat when I look from the windows of a railway carriage into suburban back gardens to see the white drawers of women hung to dry on clothes lines, and fluttering in the breeze. My imagination fills the empty galligaskins with cosy bottoms and hirsute quims. Were those drawers loquacious, like Tennyson's "Talking Oak," what mysteries might they not reveal.

A lady, putting on her riding trousers becomes,

consciously or unconsciously, akin to a hoyden assuming man's clothes, or nearer still, to a ballet girl drawing on her tights. She is subject to contact of the most perilous kind. The warm close substance that passes close to her flesh, that clasps her loins, and embraces her bum, and insinuates itself between her thighs, has, all senseless leather, cloth, or silk, as it may be, something of the nature of a man's hand in it.

Let the graces be stark naked, or vest them only with flowing drapery, and they may be as chaste as Susannah. Put them in drawers or tights and they become prostitutes.

If Diana had gone a hunting in trousers of "chamois leather with black feet," she would not have behaved, I take it, quite so savagely to poor Acteon.

And yet you may urge this Brighton schoolmistress of mine was chaste, her riding pantaloons to the contrary. So she was, as yet.

Every woman is chaste bodily until she is fucked; for frigging I look upon more as a disease than as a symptom of whoreishness.

A girl who "plays with herself" really very often does not know what she is doing; but a girl who is fucked— bar rapes and hocussing—knows perfectly well what she is about.

"In this connection," to use an American locution, allow me to relate a brief anecdote.

I had an intrigue with a married woman once (it got me into a devil of a mess in the long run), and, after tremendous difficulties, innumerable rebuffs and the most passionate solicitations, succeeded in getting her to my chambers. We had dined at Verrey's, and I had taken care to give her moselle, and not champagne; the former, when genuine (and Verrey's in those days was not the dirty hole it is now), having a subtle bouquet or aroma, very perilous to women. Moreover, I had made her "top off" with curaçoa, and in the cab which conveyed us to my chambers I took care to smoke a cigarette of the choicest tobacco of La Honradez, in Cuba. In brief, when we arrived at my chambers, by dint of lying, panting (or pretending to pant), kneeling, kissing, and dishevelling her hair, and spouting Swinbourne, I got her from a chair to sofa, and so, by erratic movements to my bedroom.

I was gently backing her on to the bed when she murmured, in a hot whisper, "Stop till I take off my drawers."

The bitch! She was determined that the washer-woman should not be a confident of our amours. Oh, woman! woman!

I was relating this agreeably characteristic story to a friend some time afterwards, when he "capped" it with the following:

"Imagine," said he, "that I once took a girl down to Hampton Court to dinner, drove her about Bushey Park, tried in vain even to take liberties with her, and could hardly snatch a kiss. I purposely missed the last train, and we were obliged to stay at an hotel. She had so far imposed on me by her resistance to my advances, that I really began to think either that she was a modest woman, or that she had her monthlies upon her.

"If she had insisted upon sleeping alone I should have let her have her way, and given the chase up in disgust. But, to my pleased astonishment, she capitulated at the last moment, and for that month at least we were man and wife.

"I noticed, just before she began to undress, that her reticule, which lay on the table, looked somewhat bulky. When she opened it, the mystery was explained. The bitch had brought a nightgown with her."

And all this time, while I have been digressing,

stately Miss Sinclair has been waiting in her riding habit. But not for me alone has the schoolmistress waited. A canter on the cliff happened to be, on the morning referred to, precisely the recreation which slim, fair-haired, wilful Miss Talbot was not anxious to enjoy.

She had caused to be smuggled in, by the boy in buttons, from the circulating library, a copy of "Guy Livingstone," and had arranged a neat little plan for reading this edifying work while Miss Sinclair was taking her canter.

Miss Cope was privy to the plot, and would aid her in carrying it out; for, let me hint, ready as the under-governess was to denounce the misdeeds of the pupils to their mistress, she was not above being bribed into conniving at the escapades of those who could afford to pay for her reticence.

Miss Talbot was abundantly supplied with pocket money; and many were the five shillings, and even the half-sovereigns, with which she had fee'd the venal Cope.

So, when Miss Talbot was bidden to go up stairs and put on her habit, the spoilt beauty pouted and sulked; flung herself on the chair by her bedside; took furtive draughts of "Guy Livingstone's" delightful but pernicious prose; then hid the book under the mattress; crammed her waving curls into a net—this was before the days of chignons—and, finally, went so far as to take off her dress and petticoats, and draw on her "chamois leathers with black feet." But she left them unbuttoned in front, and, producing "Guy Livingstone," again fell to reading.

At least half-an-hour had elapsed since she had been told to dress.

At length, Miss Sinclair, growing impatient, went up stairs to see what the girl was about. She knew Miriam

Talbot's wilful ways of old. So, flinging the end of her habit over her arm, she swept up to the "Fourth Room," the dormitory in which Miss Talbot's couch—a pretty, snouw-white, couch it was—was located, and tapped at the door with the handle of her riding whip. It was rather a long whip for a lady to use—a slender, little switch, tapering to a point, but with a somewhat substantial handle of amber.

"Miriam," she said; "Miss Talbot, are you ready? What an unconscionable time you have been, my dear."

Receiving no answer, Miss Sinclair entered the room, armed cap-a-pie, and was as astonished as vexed to find Miss Talbot half dressed, and lounging on her chair, looking very discontented. A flush of indignation rose to Miss Sinclair's cheek, and she bent her brow and bit her lip ominously.

"What is the meaning of this? why are you not ready? Do you think it respectful to me to keep your mistress dancing attendance on you for more than half-an-hour?"

"I don't want to go out riding," quoth Miriam, in a half lazy, half insolent, tone. "I'm tired; please to let me alone."

"Are you unwell?" asked the schoolmistress, in a hard voice. For aught she knew the girl might have been suddenly taken poorly.

"No, ma'm; I am not unwell."

"Then dress yourself at once, Miss."

"I would rather not. My father said I was not to ride unless I liked."

"Your father," retorted Miss Sinclair, fingering the amber handle of her whip, and softly flicking it against her habit, in a curiously ominous manner; "your father, Miss, said you were to be docile and obedient, and not mutinous and impudent. Let me have no more of this. Put on your habit this moment."

Miriam Talbot looked at her governess with affectedly sleepy eyes, yawned, but did not stir.

"Do you hear me?"

No reply.

"Then take that." The small, plump, fair hand of Emily Sinclair—did I tell you her name was Emily?—was raised, the amber handle glistened; the whip hissed through the air; there was a sharp, crackling, sound, and it fell right across the naked shoulders of Miss Miriam Talbot.

"Ai, Ai;" screamed the fair-haired mutineer starting up. She raised her arm to ward off another blow, if it were intended. It was intended—two, three, four, five, six more vigorous cuts of the whip. Two, however, fell on the girl's stays, and did not hurt her. The last fell right across her back, for the girl, now thoroughly subdued, had thrown herself on the bed, holding her face in her hands, and bellowing pitiably.

"Have you had enough?" asked Miss Sinclair; "will you disobey me again?"

"Oh, no, ma'am; no, ma'am," sobbed Miriam; "please don't flog me any more."

"I have not flogged you," returned the schoolmistress, in whose eye there was a strange lambent flame.

"I have merely given you a foretaste of what you might expect if you continued obstinate. But I tell you what, Miriam Talbot, if you don't get up and dress this very moment, I'll pull down those trousers of yours, and give you the soundest flogging, big as you are, that girl ever had."

There was that in the emphasis with which the schoolmistress spoke—there was that in her eye and on her lip that convinced Miss Talbot that Miss Sinclair was uttering no vain threat. The cuts she had received smarted woefully; but she argued sensibly, that on another part of her person they would be even more intolerable.

"I may as well save my bum, at all events," she argued to herself. So she dried her tears, washed her face in cold water, and in five minutes was dressed.

He must have been a wizard, indeed, who, strolling along the Marine Parade that morning, and meeting the handsome schoolmistress and her fair-haired pupil gracefully cantering, a groom from the livery-stable following behind, would have divined that a quarter-of-an-hour before that auburn sylph had been cowering, half naked, under the lash of a horsewhip.

As I walk behind girls in the street, watching their swaying tournure, I often wonder if, beneath all that silk, and lace, and sarsnet—beneath the several strata of crinoline, flannel and linen petticoats, drawers and chemise, there are any such things as bottoms freshly scored by rod, or whip, or cane.

Who knows? Because a young lady was whipped in the morning, it is no reason why she should not walk down Regent-street in the afternoon.

I have often had on my own arm a young lady, dressed in the first style of fashion, and who excited, I was proud to notice, the admiration of the lounging dandies in the Burlington Arcade, and this young lady, a very short time previously, I have had securely strapped down to an armchair, or to a ladder, stark naked to her drawers, those thrust wide apart, and a pickled birch, whistling over her bleeding bum. The lounging dandies would scarcely dream of that when they saw my mistress walking so mincingly.

"It is lucky, for you, Miriam," the schoolmistress observed, with grave irony, as they approached the Steyne, "that I did not carry out my threat.

"You should have ridden under any circumstances;

but your side-saddle would have been somewhat uncomfortable had my horse-whip done what it was on the point of doing."

"Don't say anything more about it, Miss Sinclair," pleaded Miriam, blushing.

She was a good-natured little soul and did not bear her governess any malice.

"I was very obstinate and naughty; and if you had flogged me as you threatened, it would only have served me right. But you won't say anything to the other girls. Will you?"

"Not a word," answered the schoolmistress. "Bygones shall be bygones. But you'll remember my horse-whip, Miriam?'"

"I shall, indeed, Madam," replied the fair-haired beauty, wriggling her shoulders.

Patient reader of mine, we have arrived at the term of our digressions, for it so happens, that this day of incipient horse-whipping of Miriam Talbot was the very one which a capricious fate had decided should convert Miss Sinclair into a flagellant, in right earnest.

When the schoolmistress and her pupil returned to Verbena House, the school mistress found her establishment in unwonted commotion. The maids were running hither and thither, and the voices of the young ladies, in defiance of the rule which prescribed silence during the hours of study, were audible from different parts of the house, mingled with the sharp authoritative tones of the governesses. Fortunately for the school's reputation it was Wednesday, and a half-holiday, so that none of the extramural professors were present to witness this subversion of discipline.

Miss Sinclair, astounded at the disturbance, hurried, all habited as she was, into the principal schoolroom, a long but lofty apartment, running back from the house into the garden, and capable of accommodating the whole fifty pupils. In this, known as the "great" schoolroom, prayers were daily read, examinations held, and solemn reprimands publicly administered. Making her way to a kind of rostrum—her own especial desk—at the upper extremity of the room, Miss Sinclair proceeded to restore order, first by ringing a little hand-bell, and then by striking her horse-whip on the desk.

"Young ladies, to your places; Mesdames les gouvernantes, to your desks," she cried, in commanding accents.

She was soon obeyed. The girls came flocking in, and took their appointed seats in silence.

Miss Everard installed herself at a desk on a line with that of the schoolmistress, but lower in construction.

Mademoiselle de la Tourelle and Fraulein Schrobbs had desks at the opposite end of the room; and Miss Cope occupied a small pulpit near the door,

"Who is absent," asked Miss Sinclair, looking round.

"No one but Miss Talbot," answered Miss Everard, "who is gone to change her dress, and little Marian Escott, who, you will remember, Miss Sinclair, you permitted to go out this morning with Fraulein Schrobbs to visit Mr. Tegg, the dentist. The poor child suffered dreadfully all last night from toothache, and it is absolutely necessary that she should have the tooth out."

"I remember," replied Miss Sinclair; "but now Miss Everard, perhaps you will be good enough to apprise me of the cause of this extraordinary disturbance."

"I am sorry to inform you, Madame," returned the head governess, "that there has been a thief in this establishment."

"A thief," echoed the amazed Miss Sinclair.

"A thief, Madam," solemnly repeated Miss Everard.

"Two of Miss Montis's gold doubloons have been stolen from her workbox."

This Miss Montis was the Creole from Cuba of whom I spoke anon; the daughter of an immensely rich slave owner and sugar planter of Matanzas. She was fifteen, very beautiful, supremely good-natured, and intensely idle. The instructions which Miss Sinclair had received with her were explicit. She was to do exactly what she liked. She had consequently had her fling of self-indulgence, and she did no harm, for, save an entire readiness to be rogered when the proper time for rogering arrived, there was no harm in Miss Montis. She was as fond of sweetstuff as though she had been five years old, instead of fifteen, and she was as innocent and well nigh as ignorant as a calf.

The guardian and banker of this child of the Antilles was a high-dried little Spanish gentleman, who occupied a counting-house in Mincing-lane, London, quite sticky with sugar, but in which the Muscovado was fortunately neutralised by that of the choicest Havana cigars.

Senor Cortes y Alfalfa, thus was he named, resided in a "swell" boarding-house in Harley-street, where he paid five guineas a week for his entertainment, and made more or less platonic love to the lady of the house, and the Indian grass widow and itinerant spinsters who were his fellow-boarders.

There is a good deal of gratuitous fucking to be got in a first-class boarding-house—if you play your cards well.

Senor Cortes y Alfalfa frequently ran down to Brighton, staying from Saturday to Monday. Then he would take his niece out in an open carriage, or dine her regally at the Bedford or at Mutton's. Miss Sinclair would often be of the party, and on one occasion the school mistress came home from one of these banquets, quite flustered with champagne. Fortunately, it was dark; nobody saw her save Dorothy, a confidential housemaid, who grinned hugely at the unwonted sight, and the schoolmistress went to bed immediately, to rise the next morning with a racking headache.

Senor Cortes y Alfalfa combined pleasure with business when he visited London-Super-Mare; for the little man was as treacherous as a monkey, and was one of the most assiduous patrons of the bawdyhouse known as "Simmy's" on the Yard. He was continually supplying Miss Montis—her Christian name was Doloris—with pocket-money, and with a great deal more of it than she had any occasion for, and among her gifts—which he did not forget, by the bye, to charge to the account of the sugar planter and slave owner at Matanzas—there was a number of gold "ounces" or doubloons, auriferous "cartwheels" so to speak, and worth, as you may be aware, about three pounds seventeen shillings a piece.

To the wealthy heiress these coins were more of the nature of playthings than of money; still, when Miss Montis discovered, on the morning when Miss Sinclair and Miriam Talbot went out riding, that two of her doubloons were missing from a pile of about eleven, which she kept loose in a desk, she raised a prodigious outcry. She could not tell whether her desk—it was not her private one—but her scholastic desk in the schoolroom, was locked or unlocked at the time of her loss. All she knew was that she had counted her doubloons on the previous evening, and that now two of them were gone.

"Who knows anything about this business—this most shocking and disgraceful business?" asked Miss Sinclair, in an awful voice.

No reply was given to the query.

"Were I like some schoolmistresses," the really indignant lady went on, "I'd flog every girl in the school, big or little"—a shudder ran through the assemblage—"until I found out the truth. You hear me, young ladies. I'd flog you one after the other, with this horse-whip"—she brought the weapon down on the desk with sharp emphasis—"until the real culprit was discovered. But I have no wish that the innocent should suffer for the guilty. I should be sorry to extract a confession by means of torture. There can be only one among you who really deserves a flogging—the thief. Let her stand forward."

Here a voice in the distance murmured, "the servants."

"Ah! yes; the servants," said Miss Sinclair, "I forgot them. Of course they must be examined, although I should be sorry indeed to find out that one of my domestics was a thief. One doesn't flog a servant who is detected in a robbery. One sends for a policeman, and gives her in charge."

"Let me remark, Madam," interposed Miss Everard, gravely, "that wishing to spare you the pain of a disagreeable operation, I at once took it upon myself, as soon as Miss Montis's loss was discovered, to examine the servants, and, assisted by Mrs. Rumble, to search their boxes thoroughly. Nothing whatever was found which could in any way compromise their character for honesty. I hope, in pursuing this investigation, that I have not overstepped my duty."

"You have done quite right, my dear Miss Everard," the schoolmistress returned. "Sorry as I should be to find a thief among my girls; the offender might prove to be a child who had no proper consciousness of the magnitude of her crime. To have been obliged to prosecute a poor servant would have been indeed painful to me."

"And I hope, Madam," pursued the head governess, in the same grave tone, "that none of your governesses are suspected to be thieves."

"You are joking, Miss Everard. I have always had, and always shall have, the most implicit confidence in your integrity. The criminal, I feel, is sitting on one of these forms, and I do not intend to quit this room until I have detected her. Governesses and young ladies, have any of you any suspicions as to the identity of the thief."

Then up rose from the lower extremity of the schoolroom, Miss Cope. "I have," she said, in a cold hard voice.

"You suspect someone, Miss Cope."

"I do, Madam."

"And whom may the person be to whom your suspicions point."

"Miss Catherine Bellasis."

And, having uttered her denunciation, Miss Cope sat down, looking vengeance, assafœtida, and strychnine, with a dash of tartar emetic, combined.

Miss Catherine Bellasis! Why she was close upon seventeen; the tallest girl in the school, and so beautiful that Miss Sinclair, although adverse to parting with a pupil so profitable, had made up her mind to write to her parents, explaining that she had readied the maximum age allowable at Verbena House, and that she must be removed.

Her father was Mr. Bellasis, Q.C., a Chancery barrister, in very large practice.

Her mother was Lady Katherine Bellasis, a daughter of the Earl of Irvine.

Kate was the belle of the school—bright, accomplished, witty, haughty, superb. She stigmatised as a thief. Proh, Pudor!

"Will you name your reasons, Miss Cope," resumed

the schoolmistress, "for bringing this extraordinary accusation against a young lady who has hitherto been a credit and an honour to the school."

Miss Cope read very plainly in this invitation the warning—"If you don't prove your case, you will be paid a quarter's salary, and sent about your business."

"My grounds of proof," replied Miss Cope, quite calmly, "are very few and simple. I saw Miss Bellasis, at ten o'clock last night, just before the elder ones retired to bed, open Miss Montis's desk and take something from it. That something chinked. That which I saw, and which I have related, I am willing to swear to in any court of justice."

"It's a lie," cried Kate Belasis, starting up.

"Silence!" thundered Miss Sinclair, "Miss Cope, may you not have been mistaken."

"I could not have been mistaken. I saw Miss Bellasis open the desk. She took something out, and there was a chinking sound as of money."

"There must be two witnesses, I think, to prove a felony," observed the schoolmistress. "At present we have only one. At all events, it is but fair to call on the accused for her defence. Miss Bellasis, are you guilty of this shameful thing?"

"I, Miss Sinclair," responded Kate, indignantly. "How can you ask me such a thing? Do I look like a thief?"

"She certainly does look like one," Miss Cope muttered to herself between her teeth. "She's as white as a sheet. I'll be whipped myself till the blood runs down to my heels if she didn't steal the doubloons."

"Catherine Bellasis," the schoolmistress went on, more solemnly than ever, "will you pledge me your word of honour, as a pupil in this school, as an English lady, that you know nothing about this affair."

Miss Bellasis did not hesitate for a moment.

"I pledge my word," said she.

"Then Miss Cope has told an untruth."

"I do not say that, she may have been mistaken."

"I was not mistaken; you lying hussey," Miss Cope began, in great heat.

"Pray be calm, Miss Cope," interrupted the schoolmistress. "We must have no calling names here. An accusation of a scandalous nature has been brought against Miss Bellasis. She has solemnly, and on her word as a lady, denied it; and, hitherto that word no one in this school has had reason to doubt. I must look elsewhere for the culprit; and if she be present I hereby give her one last chance. If she will honestly come forward, and avow her guilt, I promise not to flog her. I don't want to flog anybody. You know this is a not a school where such punishments are used. I hate the bare idea of governing my girls with the lash. Now you have my promise. The girl who confesses must, of course, be punished; but I engage that her punishment shall neither be severe nor degrading. I won't expel her. I will not even apprise her parents of her fault. Young ladies, can I say more?"

Surely Miss Sinclair could not say any more in reason; yet that which she said failed to produce the required effect. No one came forward. Full five minutes elapsed in dead silence.

"The time for clemency has passed," cried the schoolmistress, in a terrible voice. "Mind, I intend to sift this doubloon mystery to the bottom, and whoever is proved to be guilty—be she little, or be she big—I'll horsewhip her till I can't stand over her. Call in the servants; I'll have all the young ladies stripped and searched to the skin."

"She's paler than ever," muttered Miss Cope, looking at Kate Bellasis.

"Will you permit me to suggest, Miss Sinclair," here observed the head governess, "that before proceeding tho what may prove a necessary operation—a personal search—it would be as well to make a minute inspection of all the desks and workboxes belonging to the young ladies."

"Thanks for the suggestion," replied Miss Sinclair, "I will do exactly as you advise."

She rang the bell for the school-room maid, and, on that domestic making her appearance, ordered her to desire Mrs. Rumble, with the aid of the other servants, to bring all the desks and workboxes belonging to the pupils down into the school-room. While these directions were being carried out, and successive instalments of boxes were being brought in by the maids, Miss Cope, who had not ceased to watch Kate Bellasis with the utmost narrowness, fancied that she discerned an expression of relief, and even of gratification in her countenance. "You're up to some devilment, my lady; but, whatever it is, it'll come out, or my name's not Madge Cope," said the under teacher to herself.

The pile of boxes being complete, each young lady, beginning with the seniors, was in turn summoned to give up her key, and the contents of each box were closely scrutinised by Miss Sinclair, assisted by Miss Everard.

So far as the boxes of the twenty elder girls were concerned, no traces of the missing doubloons were discovered.

More than one unexpected article, however, turned up, to the apparent discomfiture of the owner. Amid all kinds of odds and ends of school girl's rubbish—letters, ribbons, valentines, broken garters, faded flowers, and soiled gloves—articles of a gravely contraband nature were found to nestle.

Thus, in Miss Hazeltine's desk—she was fourteen—there was a phial, half full of a colourless liquid, which

Miss H., on being interrogated, declared to contain eau de cologne; but which Miss Everard, uncorking the phial and applying it to her nose, pronounced to be something else. She handed it to the housekeeper for further information.

"Lord, love you, Miss," said Mrs. Rumble, after a prolonged sniff at bottle, "why, its gin."

"Gin!" Miss Sinclair was really shocked and perplexed. "What in the name of all that was aggravating could this mere child want with gin." Her mind, however, was too much preoccupied by the thoughts of Miss Montis's doubloons to allow her to take up this alcoholic mystery on the spot. She bestowed a hateful smile on the young smuggler, and, murmuring that she "would see about it," put the bottle on one side, and ordered the search to continue.

Ere long another illicit article was found; at least its illegal nature might be surmised from the start of indignation on the schoolmistress's part, when she opened a thin octavo volume, bound in red cloth, and with gilt edges, which lay at the bottom of Miss Hatherton's desk.

Miss Hatherton, daughter of the venerable Archdeacon Hatherton, of Saltcross Marsh, Kent, was next in seniority to Miss Bellasis. She was sixteen-and-a-half, and noted in the school for the demure austerity of her manners, and her great religious fervour. Only, the Rev. Arthur Philip Calvedon did not like her, and had more than once hinted to Miss Sinclair that he considered Miss Hatherton to be a designing hypocrite. She was very low church, and that fact, perhaps, had something to do with Mr. Calvedon's disparagement of her piety.

"Where did you get this book?" asked Miss Sinclair, very slowly and with enforced calmness, but trembling, evidently, with suppressed emotion.

There was no reply. Miss Hatherton turned, alternately, very white and very red; then put her handkerchief to her eyes, but said nothing. The eyes of the schoolmistress turned, mechanically as it were, in the direction of her horse whip, lying on her desk; but she restrained herself, and saying, in a low tone that "she would question Miss Hatherton further in this matter," ordered the search to continue.

"Here they are! Here they are!" suddenly exclaimed Miss Everard.

"Here they are!" echoed Mrs. Rumble.

"Yes, there they are, indeed, exclaimed Miss Sinclair, and yet in a tone less angry than sorrowful.

The famous ounces were found. And, where do you think? At the very top of the work box of little Lucy Summerfield, who was only eleven years of age, and the pet of the whole.

"Oh, Lucy, Lucy," cried the really grieving schoolmistress. "However came you to do this wicked, shameful thing?"

She clasped her hands before her, and, looked sadly at the child. She loved her, as every one else in the house seemed to do, not only for her pretty face, and winning ways, but for her goodness, and kindness, and simplicity.

She, too, was a clergyman's daughter, but of no dignitary of the church, her father being only a poor country vicar, a distant relation of Miss Sinclair's, who had taken the girl for almost nominal terms, and would gladly have taken her for nothing.

Lucy Summerfield burst into a passion of tears. "I didn't take the money. I didn't indeed, ma'am. I don't know how it came into my box."

"Don't add falsehood to theft, you bad, wicked girl."

Lucy continued to weep and wail, and protest her innocence.

"You shall be judged by your schoolfellows, Miss," went on Miss Sinclair.

"How say you, young ladies, is Lucy Summerfield guilty or not guilty of theft? Those who think her guilty hold up your right hands."

Forty-five hands were held up, among them that of Miss Bellasis.

"Now, those who think her not guilty."

Only three palms ventured to vote for the poor child's innocence. I am glad to say that they included that of Miss Montis.

"I not think she take the money," whispered the creole to her next neighbour, Miss Talbot.

"Nor I, either," said Miriam, who had likewise been on the side of acquittal.

The third voter for absolution was Miss Gallick, the pugilist.

"She doesn't look like a thief," quoth that muscular young lady, and doesn't cry like a thief."

Miss Marian Escott, you will remember, was still absent under the escort of Fraulein Schrobbs, on a visit to M. Tegg, the dentist.

The decided verdict as to Lucy Summerfield's guilt appeared anything but satisfactory to Miss Sinclair. She sat down, passed her hands across her forehead, and, for some time, seemed lost in deep cogitation. Then she rose, gathered up her habit, took her horse-whip from her desk, and turning to the now hushed and anxious assemblage said, "You heard my words as to what I would do with the guilty person in this affair. Miss Summerfield has been convicted on the clearest evidence of a most scandalous act of dishonesty, and I am about to punish her as she deserves. No young lady will presume to stir from her place, save for necessary purposes until I return. March up to my bedroom, Miss."

This last command was addressed to poor Lucy, who, weeping bitterly, but without endeavouring to reiterate a denial, which she felt would be useless, of her guilt, left the school-room, as she ordered, followed by the schoolmistress, horsewhip in hand.

More than one girl noticed that tears were slowly coursing down Miss Sinclair's cheek.

As she passed Miss Cope, however, she drew herself up, and said, sternly, "With regard to the perfectly false accusation you have chosen to bring against Miss Bellasis, for what purpose I know not, you and I, Miss Cope, must have some farther communication to-morrow morning."

"As you please. Madam," the under teacher calmly replied. "What I saw, I saw. I am quite ready to leave you, with proper notice, and have nothing to reproach myself with as to my conduct while in your establishment Appearances are, I admit, against Miss Summerfield, but remember the cup that was found in Benjamin's sack, Miss Sinclair." "A stale defence," sneered the schoolmistress, and disdaining to interchange further parley with her subordinate, she swept from the room.

Miss Cope shrugged her shoulders, and resumed her task of watching Kate Bellasis, more keenly than ever.

It may seem strange that Miss Cope should be anxious to screen any offender from punishment. She—whose chief employments were espionage and denunciation. But Miss Cope yearned for a more notable victim than poor little Lucy Summerfield. She felt, as would a boa constrictor, to which, after a fortnight's fasting, a rabbit was offered. Miss Cope had stomach for a whole goat.

The girls, left to themselves, forbidden to move, but not enjoined to silence, fell to chattering on the probable fate of the condemned girl.

"What'll Miss Sinclair to do her?" was the first eagerly asked question.

"Why," said Miss Gallick, who had voted for acquittal, "she'll have a regular right down flogging, and I'm sorry for her, poor thing. I know how hard she can hit."

At the mention of the word flogging both Miss Hatherton and Miss Haseltine were observed to move uneasily in their seats.

"Ah! you'll catch it, both of you, make no mistake, when poor Lucy's had her whacking. What was the book about, Fanny, that Miss Sinclair found in your box?" thus inquired the provocative Gallick.

"Never mind, you spiteful thing," retorted the Archdeacon's daughter, tossing her head. "It's no business of yours; and, remember, you're only one of the junior girls, and have no right to be impertinent to your elders. Besides, I'm too old to be whipped."

"Don't he too sure of that," observed Miriam Talbot, quickly, "I don't think Miss Sinclair would be very particular about ages, if she had really made up her mind to punish a girl."

"I'd tell my papa, if she was to whip me," Miss Hatherton exclaimed, arguing against her own conviction.

Miss Haseltine said nothing, but inwardly determined to tell the whole truth about the gin bottle.

"There's no great harm in what I've done," she thought, "and if Miss Sinclair is not in a very great passion, I may get off with a very long lesson."

Meanwhile the unhappy Lucy Summerfield had "marched up," as she had been bidden, to her instructress's bedroom, sobbing all the way.

Locking the door, Miss Sinclair ordered her to "stop that howling," but the tone of her voice belied the sternness of her words. Indeed, she was almost as ready to sob as Lucy herself. On her way up stairs she had been anxiously deliberating in her mind how best to accomplish the disagreeable task imposed upon her.

Punish the girl she must; but how? Should she request Miss Everard or Mrs. Rumble to whip her. No; from such a course she shrank. Both the governess and the housekeeper she feared would be mercilessly severe to the poor child. How should she whip her? On the back; no, she might injure her chest. The bottom was manifestly the only safe place on which to punish a child.

She laid down the horse-whip on her dressing-table, took the weeping Lucy on her knee, and positively kissed her. It was not a Judas's Kiss. The approaching flogging was felt by the schoolmistress to be a thing of stern necessity. She would rather have suffered the pain and shame herself. But what was she to do?

"My poor, erring child," she said, "you see to what misery you have brought me, and yourself. You are disgraced as a thief—as a pilferer of money—before the whole school. Why did you not confess while there was yet time?"

"If I'd confessed, ma'am," answered Lucy, looking firmly, though with streaming eyes, right in her governess's face, "I should still have been a thief, and still disgraced. But I didn't steal the money, and I don't know how it came into my box."

Miss Sinclair shook her head sorrowfully.

"She is obstinately wicked," she thought, "and I must flog her. Let me get the horrible task over."

Suddenly a thought seemed to deter her from commencing the punishment. She rose; rang the bell; and on its being answered by Dorothy, desired that Mrs. Rumble would come to her.

"Mrs. Rumble," she said, when the housekeeper

made her appearance, "I am about to give this bad and deceitful girl a severe whipping, but I scarcely think a horsewhip a proper implement to use to a child of her age. Have you anything else that would do?"

"I can for a cane, ma'am," replied the house-keeper; "or, stay, there's just a light, little, half-penny switch, that the boy James beats your riding-habit with."

"Bring it me, if you please," returned Miss Sinclair much relieved.

Mrs. Rumble speedily reappeared, with the cane in question, which Miss Sinclair took up, and slowly poised, in her hand.

"Will you remain here during the punishment, Mrs. Rumble?"

"With pleasure, ma'am; leastwise, there's no pleasure to me, at all. I never fit so fit to cry in all my life."

The schoolmistress looked sympathetically in the servant's face. There were tears, too running down her cheeks.

"Don't give it too hard, ma'am," the house-keeper ventured to whisper, as Miss Sinclair proceeded to lay Lucy across her knee, and to pull up her petticoats.

"Shall I pull down her drawers," Miss Sinclair asked, in an equally low tone, when the child was duly trussed.

"I wouldn't, ma'am;" answered Mrs. Rumble. "I wouldn't even open them. The cane will sting quite hard enough through her trousers; but you've no notion how it wheals the raw flesh."

Following this benevolent advice, Miss Sinclair refrained from pulling down Lucy's trousers. They were drawers which opened behind, and until Miss Sinclair considerately brought the parts together, a fair portion of the cheeks of Lucy's rosy little bottom was visible through the aperture. Her drawers closed, however, nothing but a semi spherical surface of white linen remained as a field of operation for the cruel cane.

With a deep sigh Miss Sinclair put Lucy in the proper position to receive the lash. She passed her left arm round her waist, and made a sign to Mrs. Rumble to hold her legs, if requisite.

But there was no such need. The poor little thing lay prone upon her stomach across the governess's knee, quivering, it is true, in agonised expectancy, yet perfectly quiet, and resigned, to her fate.

Miss Sinclair raised the cane, swung it, and brought it down with moderate force on Lucy's backside.

The stripe brought from her—not a scream—but a low, plaintive cry of pain.

Again the schoolmistress raised the switch, again she swung it, and it was on the point of descending when a violent knocking was heard at the bedroom

"Who is there? who dares to disturb me?" cried Miss Sinclair, releasing Lucy, and rising in a passion.

"Miss Zinglair, Matam," the voice of Fraulein Schrobbs was heard without to say, "You most led os in. Ve haf zomding mose imbordant du gommunigate."

Miss Sinclair, not wholly displeased at this interruption to the painful drama in which she was enacting the part of executioner, pulled Lucy's clothes down over her knees, placed her on a chair, and then unlocked the door.

Fraulein Schrobbs rushed into the room, accompanied by Marian Escott, with her face bound up.

"O, Miss Zinglair," she cried, "you af mate von grade misdague. You af wip dis boor tear innosent liddle cal, and it is nod zhe who af stole te money. Ach! mein Gott! it is anoder cal. Id is—"

"Who?" demanded Miss Sinclair, almost breathless—"for God's sake tell me whom."

"Miss Catherine Bellasis," answered Fraulein Schrobbs, solemnly.

"Are you sure?" asked the schoolmistress.

"As sure," answered the agitated Fraulein, "as dat I am now ztanting hier. Oh, Miss Zinglair, Miss Zinglair, I to hobe you af nod vip dat boor liddle cal Lucy Zommerfield vat af done no nod noding ad all. Tish Miss Bellasis that mos af de vip boddom. Ja wohl auf seinen Poppo. Strafen, ja und mit einer guten Ruthe."

"Tut, tut!" said Miss Sinclair. "No harm has been done to poor little Lucy, I'm glad to say."

She remembered with remorse, and so did Mrs. Rumble, that one stripe from the cane had fallen on the poor girl's bum.

"At least," she thought, "I'm glad that I didn't hit her on the bare flesh."

She took the girl up in her arms, and kissed and fondled her, and whispered her "that she would make it up to her for her cruelty."

"But you weren't cruel, dear Miss Sinclair," murmured Lucy, "you thought me a thief, and you were obliged to punish me. It was not the flogging I minded, but the thought of being suspected of such a wicked act."

Miss Sinclair had stood Lucy on chair. She had put her hand up her clothes, and was patting and smoothing her bottom under her drawers.

Although the lash had not fallen on the bare flesh she could still feel the wheal which the ratan had made.

But Fraulein Schrobbs was anxious to tell her tale, and to prove the turpitude of Miss Bellasis.

I will not inflict any more of the Fraulein's Teutonic-English on the reader, but will content myself with recording that her story resolved itself into this:

Marian Escott had been suffering frightfully from the toothache the whole of the previous night, and Fraulein Schrobbs, always good-natured, had volunteered to sit up with her.

It must be explained that it was part of Miss Sinclair's judicious system of discipline to mingle little with big girls in the bedrooms.

"When only big ones get together," she was accustomed to say, there's sure to be vice, and with a pack of little one's there's sure to be mischief or fighting."

Miss Bellasis, verging upon seventeen, occupied a compartment or "cubicle" in the room, which likewise contained the cots of little Lucy Summerfield, and of the suffering Marian Escott.

Now, towards midnight, Fraulein Schrobbs declared that she saw Miss Bellasis emerge, clad only in her night chemise, from her "cubicle," and look cautiously around.

The Fraulein feigned to be fast asleep, and, besides, she was in a part of the room whence she could see Miss Bellasis, but that young lady could not see her.

The belle of Verbena House stole noiselessly up to a chest of drawers, on which the girls' workboxes were placed, and, with a key, opened one, which, from its bright mother of pearl ornaments, the Fraulein knew well to belong to Lucy Summerfield. She placed something in the box, locked it again, went to the po, pea'd, and then tranquilly regained her couch.

This was the tale of Fraulein Schrobbs.

"But how," asked Miss Sinclair, still apparently unwilling to believe that a young lady, verging upon seventeen years of age, could be a common thief, and a traitoress to boot, "do you know that what she put into the box was the money belonging to Miss Montis."

"Vaid a bid, Matam," replied the German governess,

"led us all co town sdairs, Luzy ant all, an Mrs. Romble, if you like, come."

Miss Sinclair felt herself, for the moment, to be entirely in the hands of the Fraulein, and, desiring the housekeeper to follow her with Miss Summerfield, led the way down stairs, the Fraulein marching behind her with Marian Escott (who had had her tooth out, and was happy), and murmuring, "Waid a bid; we shall zee, Miss Pellasis."

Miss Sinclair, the moment she entered the school-room, felt that her measures must be prompt and decided.

Catherine Bellasis had been listening close to the door to what might be going on upstairs—listening with greedy ear for the screams of Lucy Summerfield under her flogging.

She had heard, instead, an agitated, sound of voices, in which that of Fraulein Schrobbs's was prominent. Her guilty conscience told her that all was discovered.

As Miss Sinclair, followed by the German, the housekeeper, and the two children, moved up the schoolroom she could see that the face of Miss Bellasis was ashy pale, and that she was trembling violently. She saw the girl rise with some desperate attempt, no doubt, to leave the room.

"Mrs. Rumble; Miss Cope;" cried the schoolmistress, "seize Miss Bellasis."

The hour of Cope's triumph had come. She sprang on her prey as a panther would spring on an antelope. Quick as thought she locked one of Miss Bellasis's arms in hers. Mrs. Rumble seized the other.

The haughty girl made some show of resistance, but the two women literally dragged her to the top of the room, and planted her in front of Miss Sinclair's desk.

The schoolmistress was still in her riding-habit, but

she had left her horsewhip up stairs. It was lucky for Kate, perhaps, that she had done so.

"Miss Zinglair," said Fraulein Schrobbs, "before you do proceet to anyding else vill you ask Miss Montis if she hafe lost anysing elst peside her two doubloons."

Miss Montis, interrogated, declared that she had also lost an old ticked, printed and yellow paper, of the Havana lottery, which had been long since drawn, and proved a blank, and that she had attached such little importance to the document that she had not thought it worth while to mention its disappearance.

"Ver goot," remarked Fraulein Schrobbs, "now vill you pe so goot as to have Miss Bellasis search, ach, ja! to de skin."

Miss Sinclair beckoned to Miss Everard, and while the head governess, kneeling down, took a firm hold of the prisoner's ankles, the schoolmistress proceeded to rifle the pockets of her dress.

There was no need to pursue the search very long. Miss Bellasis's porte-monnaie was fished forth, and in it, folded into quarters, was the lottery ticket.

The detected robber did not faint or scream, but shut her eyes, and her lips turned very blue.

"That will do," observed Miss Sinclair, with desperate calmness. "Miss Bellasis, be good enough to retire to your bedroom. Ere many hours are over we will see what can be done with a young lady of seventeen years of age who not only thieves, but also tries to get her schoolfellows flogged for crime she has herself committed."

"Forgive me," Kate stammeringly began.

"Out of my sight this moment," thundered the schoolmistress, stamping her foot. "To your bedroom, Miss. Stay—" she added, "let her be taken to the Red Room, and locked up on bread and water. Away with her, Mrs. Rumble."

When I told you there was no "whipping-room" at Verbena House, I omitted to mention that the establishment did really contain an apartment, set aside for purposes of punishment, although not necessarily of a corporal nature.

This was the "Red Room," a back bed chamber, at the very top of the house, and which took its portentous name from the fact that it was panelled to a height of about six feet from the floor with dark crimson baize.

It was used when not wanted for the confinement of a prisoner as a drawing academy by the young ladies, the red baize walls throwing into sharp relief the plaster casts from which they drew.

A small bed chamber adjoined the Red Room, which itself contained no furniture save easels, drawing boards and two or three music stools.

When a pupil was under punishment in the Red Room, the drawing academy was held in the back drawing-room.

To the penitential apartment the first-mentioned Miss Bellasis was conveyed by the housekeeper.

A couple of servants soon removed the artistic paraphernalia of the place, and brought in a common deal table and a cane-bottomed chair, together with clean sheets, washing utensils, and a chamber pot from the bedroom.

Then Mrs. Rumble, who had disappeared for a few minutes, re-entered the room, bearing a Bible and prayer book, and a tray with a French roll on a plate, and a decanter of water.

Everything was served with great neatness and elegance.

There was a clean napkin with a silver fork, and the drinking cup was Miss Bellasis's own private and particular silver mug, with her initials engraved on it.

Every new comer to Verbena House brought with her such a silver mug, together with a fork and spoon of the same precious metal.

"That's your dinner, Miss," observed the house-keeper, pointing to the bread and water, "and it's Miss Sinclair's orders that you have to learn the sixteenth chapter of the Gospel according to St. John by heart, and this afternoon Miss Cope will come and hear you say it."

With this, exit Mrs. Rumble, locking the door behind her.

Shortly afterwards, however, the door was unlocked, and Dorothy, the housemaid, came in with a clean pillowcase, which she had forgotten. As she passed out again she bent her head over Kate's shoulder, and whispered to her sorrowfully. "Oh, Miss, won't you catch it. Whatever did you go for to act so?"

"I suppose," said Kate to herself, when the maid had retired, and the door was once more fastened, "that I should be kept in this ridiculous place for a week, with long lessons to learn."

Seven days were the maximum of confinement for a culprit confined to the Red Room.

"What did Dorothy mean by saying that I should catch it?" The prisoner went on to ask herself, uneasily. "Surely Miss Sinclair would never dare—" She dared not herself finish the phrase she had commenced in her mind.

But Dorothy, the housemaid, had known very well what she meant. On the stairs, just before, Mrs. Rumble had said to her. "Mark my word; that girl will have her backside skinned before she's twenty-four hours older."

Meanwhile the justly indignant schoolmistress had set about devising measures for inflicting on the convicted thief the punishment she so richly deserved.

The question however, of the chastisement to be inflicted on an offender who had attained the comparatively mature age of seventeen, was one by no means easy to solve.

Miss Bellasis was, to all intents and purposes, a woman. She was marriageable. Only a week before this affair took place she had passed successfully—for she was a very healthy girl—through her monthly "troubles." The fact that she had done so, perhaps, gave preponderance to a particular idea of Miss Sinclair's as to her punishment.

"Long lessons; solitary confinement!" she said to herself. "Psha, she would laugh at such correction. The idea of sending for a policeman, too, were it only to frighten her, is absurd. I don't wish the private affairs of my school to be exposed. I might expel her, without disgrace; but then, perhaps, she'd go home and tell the most disgraceful falsehoods about me. No, no, I'll flog her till the blood runs down the whole school. That'll shame her and hurt her as well—the abandoned hussey—; and I'll write a note to Mr. Calvedon, and tell him what I'm going to do, and I'll ask the teachers whether they will help me to flog her. I dare say they will."

Repeatedly murmuring between her teeth, "I'll flog her; I'll flog her," and finding, it may be half unconsciously, a vague sensation of voluptuousness in the utterance of that simple word "flog," Miss Sinclair hied her to her private parlour, and penned a hurried note to the Reverend Arthur Philip Calvedon, telling him that something extraordinary had occurred, and begged him to come to Verbena House immediately, as she wished to consult him on a matter of the very highest importance.

This billet being dispatched to its destination by the hands of Stiggles, the boy in buttons, Miss Sinclair remembered that she was still in her riding gear.

Retiring to her bedroom, she took off her habit, stripped herself to the waist, and proceeded plentifully to douche the upper part of her handsome person with cold water. Then she "did" her hair, and donned a clean chemise. She then sat down, unbuttoned her riding trousers, pulled those garments together with her trim little Wellington boots, off, and invested herself with a pair of feminine cut.

"How feverish I am," she murmured, as she tied the strings of her breeches round her waist. "This whipping business seems, I know not why, to have put my blood quite in a ferment."

Yes; Miss Sinclair was feverish. Yes, her blood was in a ferment. She felt hot between the thighs. She had detected, by touch, a slight dampness there; so straddling across her bidet, she laved the hot, moist parts with water, in which she had put a few drops of Baily's toilet vinegar.

The application refreshed her; but still her blood was mutinous, and there were singings in her ears, and "flog, flog, flog; whipping flogging," echoed and re-echoed in her mind. And, although she was too refined a lady to express, even mentally, such coarse and vulgar words as "arse," "bottom," "backside," "bum," or even "posteriors," there was, nevertheless, continually present to her mind's eye the vision of a tall girl, naked from the waist downwards, and struggling, kicking, and screaming under a lash, every vibration of which raised crimson stripes on her bare flesh.

The young ladies had by this time dined, and were now in the full enjoyment of their half-holiday. That is to say, they were playing or gossiping in the schoolrooms or the playground, comme bon leur semblaient; but in accordance with Miss Sinclair's directions, no young lady had left the house.

She could not spare any of the teachers, having convened a council of war of those ladies to debate the momentous question of the—how, when, and where of Miss Bellasis's punishment.

The council met in her private sanctum—the back drawing room, which was furnished half a library and half as a boudoir.

"Ladies," she begun, when the whole corps of governesses had assembled, "You are aware of the scandalous events of this morning. I have made up my mind to inflict on Miss Bellasis a punishment which shall be at once exemplary and severe—an ignominious punishment—an unusual one, perhaps, but still one which I consider that, under the circumstances, I am justified in inflicting. Ladies, I mean to give her a thorough flogging."

A murmur of approval ran round the board.

"Before the entire school."

Renewed symptoms of acquiscence.

"As to the exact manner of the chastisement," went on the school mistress, "I must seek your advice. What do you say, Miss Everard?"

"I say, Madam," replied the senior governess, "that you have made up your mind to do a very wise and energetic thing. Let this young lady be flogged by all means; but, if you will allow me to proffer advice, don't flog her with your riding whip. The flogging to be efficacious must be severe. Thus, I think Miss Bellasis should be made to bear at least four dozen or fifty cuts. Now four dozen lashes with a horsewhip would so mark her person that the effort might be apparent for very many weeks. The same objection would apply to a cane, a strap, or a rope."

"I've seen a gutta percha whip used," Miss Cope ventured to observe, "in the institution where I was brought up, and it almost cut pieces out of a girl's—"

She was going to say "bottom," but pulled up, and substituted "back."

"Je suis de l'avis de Mademoiselle Everard," remarked Mdlle. la Tourelle, to whom Miss Sinclair next appealed for her opinions, "Sans doute cette jeune personne mérite une punition très sévère. Dans les pensionnats de demoiselles en France les peines corporelles n'existent pas. Le purtt, la verge, tout cela a été aboli par la Révolution. Je ne dis pas que la cause de la morale en ait beaucoup profité. Madame Campan, dans le temps a fessé les sœurs de Napoléon, et l'Empereur, qui n'aurait pas consenti à ce qu'un soufflet fut donné dans les Lycées ou dans sa maison Impériale de St. Denis, souriait quand Madame parlait d'avoir tenu les Reines Hortense et Caroline "sous la verge." Mais vous me permettrez l'observation que bien qu'une demoiselle de l'âge de Mdlle. Bellasis ne serait point punie corporellement dans une institution d'éducation séculaire le honteux délit commis par elle amènerait certainement sa réclusion dans une maison de correction. Elle irait chez les Sœurs Girsco, ou dans quelqu'autre communauté renommée pour la sévérité de sa discipline; et là, je vous garantis, on ne la ménagerait pas. A dix-sept ans nonobstant on la sanglerait, soit avec une verge de bouleau, soit avec un martinet sur une partie de son corps nu que la pudeur m'empêche de nommer: et cela, non pour de nouvelles offenses par elles commis mais deux on trois fois par semaine régulièrement et comme par ordonnance du médécin. J'ai bien connu une demoiselle de grande maison qui a été fustigée de la sorte trois fois dans chaque quinzaine pendant six mois....."

"Qu'est-ce que c'est que le martinet dont vous parlez Mademoiselle?" asked Miss Sinclair, seemingly much interested in these penitential details.

"C'est un manche de bois au bout duquel est cloué

une douzaine de lanières de cuir coupées carrément. Au besoin on fait des nœuds aux bouts de ces lanières. Pour de très petits enfants ces étriviéres sont en peau de daim, molle comme celle d'un gant, et le martinet ne peut être considéré que comme un purt pour rire; mais, dans les couvents et les maisons de correction, la chose prend une allure bien différente. Le cuir est dur aux aigus et ses nœuds sont comme du fer. Quelquefois les lanières sout bouillies dans du lait pour leur donner plus de raideur précisément comme ou fait avec le knout Russe. J'ai vu le dos et les fesses—excusez moi le mot—des filles déchiré et découpé en vrais lambeaux de chair par ces terribles instruments. Il y a aussi un autre martinet composé de cordes tressées et ayant trios nœuds chacune. C'est un purt qui figure beaucoup plus que le martinet du cuir, et qui fait jaillir le sang assez promptement mais qui n'inflige pas les graves ecchymoses du martinet de cuir. En Angleterre jamais je n'ai vu un martinet quoique j'ai souvent entendu parler du "cat-o-nine tails" avec lequel sont punis les soldats anglais. Mais votre chat n'a que neuf queues tandis que le nôtre en a douze. Je suppose que vous n'avez pas l'intention d'attacher Miss Bellasis aux hallebardes et de lui donner du "chat" sur le dos, comme à un troupier qui aurait dérobé quelque chose à ses camarades, mais que vous voulez lui donner le purt comme à un enfant. Et vraiment elle n'est qu'une grande enfant et mérite d'être traitée comme telle. De la cravater serait peut-être cruel. Troussez la jupe, prenez une bonne verge, et fessez la jusqu'au sang. On trouvera bien moyen de la lier ou de lui tenir les bras et les jambes si elle résite."

"Par fesse, Madlemoiselle," interposed Miss Sinclair, "vous voulez conseiller qu'elle serait punie."

"Mon Dieu, Madame, puisque nous sommes en petit

conseil de femmes on peut dire la chose vertement par 'fesse' je veux dire sur le cul. On ze behind, Madame, vat you call ze bom."

Miss Sinclair nodded her head. She was past the blushing stage.

"On her bare bottom," she went on with new found decision. "I mean to pull her petticoats up and flog her till the blood runs down her heels. Are you of a similar opinion, Fraulein Schrobbs?"

"She deserfe de vip," quoth that young lady, "and I hope you gif her de vip as art as you vos goin tu gif id tu boor little Loozy Zommerfield."

"Never fear; she shall have it," replied the schoolmistress. "Miss Cope, have you anything to say?"

"Only this, Madam, that you'll find it rather a difficult job to flog Miss Bellasis. She's as strong as a young lioness. It'll take all the teachers to hold her, and I shouldn't wonder if she bit and kicked as well."

"She shall be tied down," cried Miss Sinclair, sternly.

She rang the bell, which was answered by Mrs. Rumble, who guessed that her services would speedily be required.

"Mrs. Rumble," began the schoolmistress, "I shall give Miss Bellasis a severe flogging—a public flogging—to-morrow morning after breakfast. I shall flog her with a birch-rod. Do you know what a birch is?"

Mrs. Rumble curtsied, and said that she did.

"You must have two, ma'am," she added, "in case of need; and I must get 'em at once, for they must be kept in soak all night."

"I leave the matter entirely in your hands," returned Miss Sinclair. "But stay; Miss Cope has hinted that resistance may be expected from Miss Bellasis. It may be necessary to tie her down to a desk or form. You had better provide straps or cords in view of such a contingency."

"I'll see about it, ma'am," responded Mrs. Rumble. And so, Miss Sinclair rising, and making a grave inclination of the head to her assistants, the flogging council of war was broken up.

It was time, for the quick ear of the school mistress had caught the sound of a double knock, the timbre of whose verberations she knew full well, at the front door, and the governesses had scarcely left the room before the Rev. Mr. Calvedon was announced.

On him the schoolmistress rarely failed to bestow her sweetest smiles, but on the present occasion her graciousness was mingled with a kind of nervous mauvaise honte.

She found herself blushing and trembling, she knew not why; and had any one then possessed the inestimable privilege of sliding his hand up Miss Sinclair's thighs, he might have found that the thicket which tufted the base of her abdomen was bedewed with a strange warm moisture.

Arthur—one may as well call him Arthur in future— could not help noticing the unusual agitation of the handsome schoolmistress, and, with an expression of genuine interest in his voice, asked if she was ill.

"N—n—no," Miss Sinclair replied, "but sadly upset by a very distressing event in my school. To tell the truth my nerves are completely shattered."

"And how hot your hand is," remarked Arthur. "Have you sent for Mr. Jossop? Really, my dear Miss Sinclair, you must take care of yourself."

"I think," interposed Miss Sinclair, "that some sensible advice will do me more good than all Mr. Jossop's physic, and it is counsel I must seek from you, Mr. Calvedon."

"You know that you can command me in anything

and everything. I am all attention."

"Thank you," the schoolmistress went on. "Now don't be startled at what I am going to say although it may appear to you indecorous; nay, almost indelicate."

"Go on, my dear Madam; a priest and a doctor are—as you know—father confessors."

Arthur began to feel oddly interested. Some piquant revelation was evidently about to be made.

Had the boy in buttons—the precociously profligate Stiggles—been caught in bed with one of the young ladies? Had one of the governesses eloped with the drawing master? His curiosity was soon satisfied.

"I am about," pursued Miss Sinclair, casting her eyes down, and playing with the trinkets of her watch, "to take a very bold, and, with me, an unusual step with one of my pupils in a matter of scholastic discipline. Mr. Calvedon a shameless act of theft has been committed in this school. The criminal, to her infinite dishonour, endeavoured to fix her own guilt on a younger schoolfellow. I was about to punish the poor little thing as one would punish a child—in fact I took her up to my bedroom to whip her, when, providentially, as I may say, the real culprit was unmasked. That culprit, Mr. Calvedon, was Miss Catherine Bellasis."

She went on to tell the astonished clergyman the whole story of Miss Montis's lost doubloons, of their discovery in Lucy Summerfield's workbox, and of the ultimate éclaircissement brought about by Fraulein Schrobbs.

"Mr. Calvedon," she continued, "such gross and hardened wickedness on the part of Miss Bellasis demands, in my opinion, and all my governesses concur with me, the severest chastisement. It demands a punishment not only a correction to the sufferer, but a warning and example to her schoolfellows."

"I agree with you thoroughly," said Arthur.

"Looking at the case in this light," went on Miss Sinclair, "I have determined, Mr. Calvedon, to give Miss Bellasis a sound flogging with a birch rod, before the entire school."

"Pardon me," Arthur responded, "I think the very best thing you could do with so wicked a girl is to flog her soundly; and some degree of publicity might advantageously be attached to the castigation. But were I in your place I would only allow the elder girls to be present at the flogging. If the birch is properly administered, some blood must necessarily be split—I speak from old public school experience—and the girl's person will exhibit a shocking spectacle before the punishment is over. Then she will probably scream, and make use of very improper language; and, altogether, the sight may be one calculated to terrify the younger children, and cause some of them to faint away."

"And the elder ones," inquired Miss Sinclair, with a half smile, "might they not also swoon at unwonted spectacle of a birching?"

"Any such symptoms may be very easily obviated," Arthur returned, "by a simple intimation on your part that the birch has been recommended by your medical man as an infallible cure for syncope, and that any young lady who chooses to faint away will be restored to consciousness by a smart application of the rod. My dear Madam, women can bear the sight of blood much better than men can. Ask the butcher's wife? Ask the hospital nurse? But I forget; you must know whether I am right or wrong."

"I shall not enlighten you on the subject," replied Miss Sinclair. "But I think there is no danger of my fainting away at the sight of a few drops of blood on a naughty girl's back."

"Not on her back, not for worlds, my dear Madam," Arthur said, quickly, and holding up a warning finger. "To a girl of Miss Bellasis's age flogging on the shoulders, or in the region of the waist, might be fraught with the very gravest perils. Really, you must pardon me, if I speak to you as a medical man would do. The cervical vertebræ, the bones at the back of the neck, are exceedingly sensitive. A succession of blows there may kill; and, in view of this, soldiers, when they are flogged, are permitted to retain their leathern stocks. Again, when the twigs of the birch are long and supple, they will often attain the front part of the person, and all kinds of injuries might result from a blow reaching the breast. The part appointed by nature, my dear Miss Sinclair, for corporal punishment, is the lower portion of the person—below the loins—the top, back part of the thighs, in short—"

"Or," Miss Sinclair added, blushing crimson, but, laughing, "that part of the body which is called, more briefly still "the bottom." There, we are old friends, Mr. Calvedon, and may speak in plain English. You think that Miss Bellasis should be flogged on the bottom. I agree with you; and it was only through a ridiculous feeling of privacy that I spoke of her back. But it is now that I wish your public school experience to come to my rescue. How am I to set about this task? I have asked my governesses, but have no great faith in their competence to advise me."

"Well, my dear Madam, there is a considerable difference between the form of flogging a boy and flogging a girl. In the first instance you have but to order the offender to pull trousers down. Then you have him hoisted on another boy's back, or you cause him to kneel across a desk, or to lie across a form. At Eton there is the "block" a kind of bed-steps. At some grammar schools they have a "horse," something between a block and an easel. In schools where the birch is frequently used the boys scarcely ever require to be held down. They take their flogging as a matter of course. All that is requisite is that a boy should stand by to hold up their shirt."

"Well, Mr. Calvedon, I don't see such a vast difference between the two cases. A boy, you say, must have his trousers pulled down. A girl wears drawers, and they must also be pulled down before she is punished."

"Not necessarily, my dear Miss Sinclair. My sisters used frequently to be whipped by their mamma, and I have often witnessed the punishment; but I never saw their drawers pulled down, they were merely opened behind. Granting, however, that you wish Miss Bellasis to have the full benefit of the birch—"

"I do," observed Miss Sinclair, significantly.

"Under those circumstances then, her drawers being completely removed, another operation has to be gone through. Her clothes must be pulled up."

"Not so, I intend to put her to the more shame, by stripping her naked, that is to her chemise and stockings."

"Then I don't see what further difficulties lie in your way."

"Pardon me. She will not take her flogging coolly, and as matter of course, as Eton boys do. She will undoubtedly struggle, and, perhaps, kick.

"You spoke of "hoisting" just now. What is it? and could such a plan as that be managed?"

"Scarcely, with this particular patient. The person who 'hoists' is generally the biggest and strongest boy in the school, and sometimes he is a man servant kept for the express purpose. You have read it, "Tom Jones"? Yes; of course you have. We have all read it.

When the Reverend Mr. Thwackum designed to flog Tom Jones he was accustomed to send for one of Squire Allworthy's footmen, and it was on the back of that retainer that the young gentleman was elevated to be birched. I know a lady in Devonshire who kept a footman to carry out in fact that which Fielding has told us in fiction. She had five sons, and I have known her flog the whole five in one morning—lads ranging between ten and sixteen years of age."

"Had she any girls?" Miss Sinclair asked, eagerly.

"Yes; two, my dear Madam, and very fine girls they were."

"Did she ever flog them?"

"Frequently; but I need not say that the co-operation of the footman was dispensed with in their case. She used to punish them in the bedroom of her lady's maid, or of her governess. But we are wandering from the subject A culprit to be hoisted or horsed places his wrists in the grasp of the official who stands before him; and who, thereupon, stooping, lifts him off the ground, in a position from which, if the hoister is strong, the boy hoisted can not budge an inch. The particular part of the person to be operated upon—the bottom—is placed with mathematical nicety in the direct way of the birch, and every blow tells. But very rarely do you find a woman strong enough to hoist even a middling sized girl without staggering. She might carry her pick-a-back, but in hoisting the whole weight of the culprit's body hangs from the wrists, I don't think that even Mrs. Rumble, strong as she looks, could hoist Miss Bellasis properly. After a few lashes she would be obliged to let her down. She would, probably, try to kick her."

"I'd have her legs held."

"Well, she might bite her shoulders."

"I'd have her gagged."

"There would be a risk in that case of her breaking a blood-vessel. My advice is, in cases of flogging, to allow the sufferer to bawl as much as he or she likes. Is there any danger of Miss Bellasis's screams under punishment being heard?"

"Not the slightest. This is a corner house, you know; the schoolroom is at the back, and from my only neighbour, Mrs. Colonel Gervoise, I have, I fancy nothing to fear, Indeed, I shall pay her a visit this evening, and tell her what is about to take place. Unless I am very much mistaken she has somewhat advanced ideas regarding discipline. At all events, she told me that she whipped her own children, and has often advised me to use the rod with my pupils."

"You have commenced very late, dear Miss Sinclair," said Arthur, "but it strikes me that you are in a way to make up very adequately for all shortcomings, but you can't have Miss Bellasis horsed or hoisted, you see. The terms are synonymous. You have no block, in your establishment. Miss Bellasis might be made to kneel on a pair of bedsteps it is true; but they would be too short—she is the tallest young lady in your school, and she would, perhaps overturn them altogether. Of her being made to lie full length on a form I do not approve. I think she would feel the birch more acutely if she assumed a kneeling or arched position. You have a large desk in the school-room, have you not?"

"Certainly."

"Well, make her lie across that, resting her knees on a stool. If she struggled her hands and feet can be held. If she is too violent for her holders you can tie her to the legs of the desk. And, above all, my dear Miss Sinclair, when you flog strike home, there is nothing like it. Avoid her back, her thighs, and her legs. Let your target always and invariably be the centre of her bottom."

With this parting advice, Arthur, squeezing the schoolmistress's hand, and devoutly wishing that he could be privileged to witness the flogging of which he had assisted in arranging the preliminaries, rose to go.

"One moment more," said Miss Sinclair. "Mrs. Rumble is preparing the rods. She says they must lie in soak all night. Is that correct?"

"Perfectly so. Mrs. Rumble is a treasure."

"How many cuts? dear Mr. Calvedon."

"Hum; Miss Bellasis is strong. My dear Madam, I should advice you not to fix any number arbitrarily. First flog her till in your own sound discretion you think it prudent to leave off. Nothing under three dozen, however, will draw blood."

"Miss Everard said four dozen, or fifty cuts," Miss Sinclair remarked, musingly.

"Miss Everard probably speaks from experience; but is the trial only that will prove the fact. Some girls would stand a hundred lashes with a birch, and others would be half killed with a dozen stripes. I think Miss Bellasis possesses a reasonable share of fortitude. And now, dear Miss Sinclair, I must really say good bye."

Very reluctantly did the schoolmistress allow the clergyman to depart. A dozen times she had been on the verge of asking him to inflict the flogging himself, in private.

She pictured to herself Miss Bellasis stripped and bound to an easy chair in her boudoir, and Arthur standing over her plying the scourge on her rapidly reddening bottom.

The girl, she reasoned, would be ashamed to tell her parents that she had been flogged by a man. But then, she remembered, that she was pledged to her governesses to the solemn and public administration of the punishment.

The news of the coming execution was probably spread by this time through the school. Not only voluptuousness, but the vindictiveness of justice craved satisfaction. She abandoned the design with respect to Arthur when, fortuitously, she remembered the cases of Miss Haseltine and Miss Hatherton.

"Do you mind coming to-morrow," she whispered, "when all is over? I shall have something very particular to speak to you about."

Arthur very gladly promised to call in Sussex-square the next day at noon, and so, with one more squeeze of the hand, took his leave.

It was Mrs. Rumble, the housekeeper, who was in waiting in the hall to let him out. She dropped a low curtsey as she saw him descending the stairs. The housekeeper and he were old cronies.

"So, Mrs. R.," he whispered, "there's to be a turning up of tails in this establishment to-morrow morning."

Mrs. Rumble nodded her head.

"It will be a performance," she remarked.

"Have you got the rods?"

"Yes, Sir; such stingers. They'll fetch the blood in no time. We shall have rare work with her; but she'll catch it—of that you may be sure."

"I shouldn't mind seeing it myself," said Mr. Calvedon, selecting his umbrella from the stand.

"That might be managed, Sir," said the house-keeper, in the lowest of tones. "If you didn't mind coming very early—say eight o'clock—and only ring the bell, instead of knocking, I could pop you into a closet, in the schoolroom, and you could have a beautiful view of the whole affair, from first to last."

END OF I^{te} VOLUME.

The

Mysteries of Verbena House

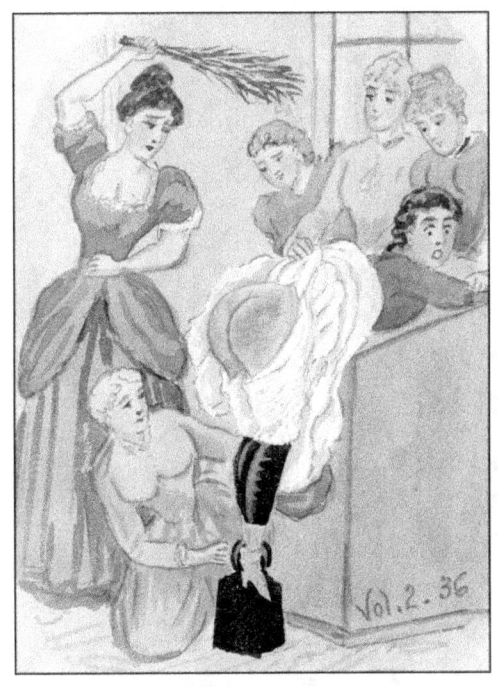

TOME II

BIRCHED FOR THIEVING,

OR

THE PUNISHMENT OF MISS BELLASIS.

On more than one occasion, but not at Verbena House, had the discreet Mrs. Rumble ministered to the peculiar penchants of the Reverend Arthur Philip Calvedon, than whom no more inveterate, and no more scientific flagellant existed, in the select community of backside-birchers.

Mr. Calvedon, however, on the present occasion declined the housekeeper's hospitable invitation.

"No, thank you, Mrs. R.," he said, as he passed from the hall. "I've other business to attend to to-morrow morning. Not far from here, however, and I shall call on Miss Sinclair at twelve precisely. Good bye, Rumble."

"Ah! I think I can guess his business," said the housekeeper to herself, as she closed the door.

"Catechism with those children of Mrs. Gervoise, next door. Tally reports of conduct. Miss Amy's bum smarted. Miss Lily served the same; Master Herbert caned. Ah! Mr. Calvedon, he knows how to enjoy himself. I don't think he cares about big girls, and that Kate Bellasis is surely a wopper to have to do with. How she'll bellow, to be sure. But I must go and look after the birch."

And yet Arthur was half sorry, as he walked away, that he had not played into the housekeeper's hand.

"A girl of seventeen birched till the blood runs! That's something that ought to be a tit-bit," he mused.

"No," he resumed, "it would be a row. I'd sooner see a girl of ten across her mother's knee, and smacked with a slipper. Why, I'm sure I don't know. Upon my word I don't think Rumble needed to have troubled herself. There was something in Miss Sinclair's eye that seemed to say, "ask; and I will refuse you nothing." A fine woman, that schoolmistress. This is her first birching, but it won't be the last, or I'm very much mistaken."

Thus silently thought the Reverend Mr. Calvedon, of whom, more anon.

Mrs. Rumble, in the interim, was not idle. According to her instructions, Dorothy, the confidential housemaid, had proceeded in the course of the afternoon to a neighbouring oil shop, and had there demanded two new sixpenny birch besoms.

"Are they for sweeping up the wash'us, or for giving one of your girls a hidin'?" asked Mr. Lippincott, proprietor of the oil shop in question.

"Go along with you," cried the outraged Dorothy, "hidin', indeed. Do you think we keep a charity school? Let me have the besoms, and none of your nonsense, Mr. Lippincott."

"Yes; but Dolly," urged the gallant oilman, pressing

some figs into the housemaid's palm, "I must know, my dear, elst how can I execute the horder. There's besoms and besoms. See here; them's odly for housework, stubby, broomy, heather. Now these— long, hard, brown, twiggy, ones—is what we call tickle-tobies. They only want undoing and tying up in bunches and they're fit for use. See they're full of buds. These is the tickle-tobies I sells to Dr. Swisher, of Scrubtail-terrace, and Mr. Brusher of the Anglo-French College on the 'ill, and lots of private families where they'ers plenty of children. Now which of the two does your missis want, Dolly?"

"If you must know," returned the housemaid, thus hard pressed, "these," and she pointed to the long, hard, brown, twiggy, besoms, which Mr. Lippincott had characterised as tickle-tobies.

"Of course, I thought so," cried the astute oilman. "Why didn't you say so before? Spare the rod, and spoil the child; eh, Dolly? But look you here. Don't you go carrying these here birch besoms through the street. You'll be chaffed to death by the boys. My young man shall bring 'em round, done up in a piece of sacking."

And in the course of half-an-hour the two birch besoms, thus prudently disguised, were left at the rear gate of Verbena House.

"There's yer hinstruments of torchur, Mrs. R.," said Stiggles, the boy in buttons, to the housekeeper, who had come down specially to the kitchen to receive the besoms. "There they are;" and Stiggles threw the mass of birch in the most irreverent manner on the kitchen dresser.

"Never you mind. Sir," retorted the housekeeper, indignantly. "If I had the ordering of you I'd have your breeches down in a jiffy, and one of these birches laid across your backside."

"But you musn't, Mrs. Rumble," the unabashed Stiggles went on. "It'ud be a hassault. Miss Sinclair musn't touch me, nor you neither, and I don't care for your old birch besoms, not that," and Stiggles snapped his fingers.

Stiggles knew as well as anybody else in Verbena House—save, perhaps, the person most nearly concerned, and she had a very shrewd inkling of the truth—that, on the following morning, Miss Bellasis would be flogged. There was no reticence as to the locality of the chastisement among the servants.

"She'll have it on her arse," quoth the cook, shortly. "I wouldn't be in her skin for something."

"Does the birch hurt, cook?" asked one of the housemaids.

"How should I know, stoopid?" returned cookey. "I never had nothing but the strap across my rump."

Disdaining to take part in this ignoble conversation, Mrs. Rumble had retired with her birchen store into the back kitchen, where, with the assistance of the scullerymaid, she set about manufacturing Mr. Lippincott's tickle-tobies into rods.

The first step was to remove the besom-sticks from the mass of twigs. Having cut the ligature which bound them together, Mrs. Rumble picked out from the mass of birch a sufficient number of the longest and most bristling twigs and which were the fullest of buds.

These she very carefully formed into bundles, binding the handles tightly with whipcord.

To be quite on the safe side, for accidents will happen at the best regulated floggings, she made three, in lieu two rods, as she had originally designed.

Very formidable instruments they were; and not in vain had Mr. Lippincott vaunted the scholastic qualities of his "tickle-tobies."

Each of the rods was about two-feet-and-a-half long. At the handle it might with ease be grasped by a lady, but at the upper extremity it had a much wider circumference; at least eight inches diameter extending on every side in branching sprays.

But this was only the first stage of preparation.

"They're all very well to look at as they are," observed Mrs. Rumble to the scullerymaid Sarah. "But, bless you, they'd be no good to flog with. They'd break short off, they're so brittle; and we should have the whole schoolroom littered with bits of birch. No, no; I must give them a pickling."

Mrs. Rumble accordingly put the rods into the sink, turned on the cock, and gave them the benefit of a full stream of water for about ten minutes; then she very carefully dried them with a rough towel.

Sarah had in the meantime prepared a pail of water, into which she had put, by Mrs. Rumble's directions, a pound of soda, two pounds of salt, and a quart of vinegar.

"Rods come expensive," quoth the housekeeper, with a grim smile, as she laid her scourges in brine. "What with one thing and another these do come to close on half-a-crown; but what's that in a first-rate finishing school. I suppose Miss Sinclair'll charge for them in her bill. There now, Sarah, we'll leave the pretty things to soak all night; and in the morning they'll be as fresh as paint, and as hard as iron, and as supple as whalebone. They'll fetch pieces out of young Madam's bum, I'll warrant you."

And with this the housekeeper retired.

Sarah, the scullerymaid, left alone, took one of the birches out of the pail, swung it round to free it from some of the superabundant moisture, and holding forth one of her brawny palms, brought the rod down upon it at what a steamboat engineer might call "half speed."

"Goodness, gracious," cried the girl, wincing, "doesn't it sting! Fancy a dozen cuts with that on the bare cheeks of your arse."

"A dozen," contemptuously repeated the cook, who had entered the scullery. "Miss Bellasis will have four dozen, as hard as Miss Sinclair and Miss Everard can give it her. They're to take turn and turn about. The foreigners ain't to be allowed to flog, because they're too soft hearted, and as to Miss Cope, missus daresn't trust her with the birch, because she's so spiteful, and hates Miss Bellasis so. Praps she'd cut her between the legs, and so do her an hinjury."

"If one of them twigs caught me on my fe-for-shame," observed Dorothy, the confidential, "I think it would make me feel funny."

"Shall I try?" asked the cook, seizing one of the rods from the pail.

"No—no—no," cried Dorothy, holding down her clothes with both hands, and retreating into a corner. "Turn her up!" cried Madam Cook, brandishing the rod.

Sarah and another servant maid seized hold of the half-laughing, half-terrified Dorothy; dragged her into the kitchen; threw her across the table, and pulling up her petticoats, revealed a remarkably plump white bottom.

The girl wore no drawers, and her legs were clad in black cotton stockings. Her underlinen was, however, scrupulously clean, and, simple as was the sight, it might have aroused a pleasurable sensation in the amateur, blasé with more luxurious flogging spectacles.

I have sometimes derived more gratification from an impromptu smart bottom than from the most elaborate performance, with all its concomitants of pickled rods, velvet-covered horses, crimson leather straps, and masked executioners.

There are seasons when a mutton chop is worth all the suprèmes de volaille in the world.

Dorothy's white bottom, exposed like a cream cheese in a clean cloth, made the cook lick her lips. She raised the birch and brought it—not cruelly—but lovingly down on the smooth and elastic surface, drawing the twigs leisurely across the cheeks, and then filliping with the ends the hairy recesses of Dorothy's privates.

"Does that make you feel funny?"

"Yes, cook; it does."

Another stroke.

"Does that?"

"Yes; a little harder!"

"Is that hard enough ?"

"A—a—ow!" and Dorothy jumped up with a half shriek. "That's too hard, cook. I didn't think you would be so spiteful."

"Lor, bless you," said the cook, grinning, as she replaced the birch in the pail, while Dorothy smoothed down her disordered garments. "Miss Bellasis'll have it ten times harder than that. But, I'll tell you what, girls, when the thing comes off to-morrow, we'll all have a peep. We can easily see through the schoolroom door ajar."

"Me, too, Mrs. Joynter?" asked the irrepressible Stiggles, appearing at this conjuncture from the upper regions.

"That boy'll be the death of me," cried the cook, "Will you hold your tongue, and mind your own business? you young varmint. If you don't, as sure as you're alive I'd let your mother know what a worrit you are, and she'll tan your hide for you. I wish she'd let missus give you a birching when she's done with Miss

Bellasis."

Whereat Stiggles grinned in a defiant manner, but prudently subsided into silence. I say prudently; for Stiggles's mamma was a washerwoman, of considerable muscular power, and of constitutional warmth of temper, occasionally aggravated under the influence of the wash tub and the gin bottle, to ferocity. More than once had she gone to the length of stripping her son and heir as naked as he was born, and tying him up, in that nude state, to her mangle, belabouring him with a rope or a strap until his body from the nape of his neck to his heels was black and blue.

Leaving the rods in pickle, and the servants to gossip on their proximate employment, I must return to Miss Bellasis, whom I left in strict captivity in the Red Boom, studying that portion of St. John's Gospel which had been allotted to her as a penitential task.

She had a very good memory, and by the hour, about five o'clock, when Miss Cope arrived to hear her repeat the chapter, she was letter perfect.

Miss Cope did not condescend to bestow any praise upon her for her proficiency.

"You'll have some more bread and butter for supper," she remarked, coldly; "If you have any appetite for it? I'm sure I couldn't swallow a morsel if I were in such a situation of shame and disgrace."

"You needn't insult me," Kate remarked, in a low voice.

"Insult you! bah! Insults are wasted upon such a creature as you," returned the malevolent Cope. "I don't think you are going to crow over me any longer, Kate Bellasis. I've stood your insolence and arrogance too long. You're a very grand young lady, no doubt, and your father's a Q. C., and very rich, and I'm only a poor under-teacher in a boarding-school; but I'm not a liar, and I'm not a thief, Miss Catherine Bellasis."

"Spare me!" groaned the wretched girl. "I must have been mad—mad, when I did it."

"Oh! I daresay, mad; but Miss Sinclair's got a cure for madness. Do you know how you're going to be brought to your senses to-morrow morning?"

"N—n—o!"

"I dare say its a lie, and that you've guessed it; but if you haven't, I'll tell you. This is what's going to be done with you. You're going to be flogged, Miss Catherine—whipped with a birch-rod, like a child. You—a great big thing of seventeen. Think of the shame! Your clothes will be turned up—I shouldn't wonder if Miss Sinclair had you whipped stark naked. And your fine ladyship's bottom is going to be cut and slashed with a great besom till the blood runs. Aha! it'll smart, I promise you; and all the big girls will be present to see the grand Miss Bellasis—, Birched for thieving."

Cope rather hissed than spoke these words, glaring meanwhile at the captive with hateful eyes.

"I'd kill myself first," cried Kate, starting up, and pushing her hair from her temples with both hands. Her forehead throbbed as thought it would have burst.

"I'll kill myself. Flogged—flogged like a charity girl! never."

"Charity girls are not flogged so often as you think for," Miss Cope resumed, with bitter scorn. "Charity girls have all sorts of people to interfere in their behalf. The servants in this house would rise in rebellion if it was a girl in their own class in life who was to be punished. But they'll quite rejoice when its a haughty young lady who is to be birched. They would all help to hold you down, or to flog you, if they were asked. They hate you; so do I. I'd give a quarter's salary to have my will of you for five minutes with one of the rods that are soaking down stairs in pickle. Do you hear that?"

"In pickle!"

"The birches are being steeped in brine, that they may cut the sharper. You won't be able to sit down again for a week."

"Mercy! mercy!" sobbed Miss Bellasis.

"I'd have as much mercy on you as you had upon Lucy Summerfield, when, through you, Miss Sinclair took her up stairs to whip her with a cane. I'd have as much mercy as I hope Miss Sinclair and Miss Everard will have upon your bum to-morrow morning, when they cut into it with the birch. I could show you a little mercy now, but I won't. I could give you some alum dissolved in water, and if you washed your bum with that to-night, and let it dry, the birch wouldn't hurt half as much. But you shall feel every stripe of it."

"I tell you," Miss Bellasis cried, despairingly, "that I will kill myself before one abhorrent lash is laid upon me."

"No you won't; no you won't," returned Miss Cope, with a smile that was perfectly fiendish. "Miss Sinclair thought of that little contingency, and has given me full instructions how to act. Dorothy, the maid, will come and sit with you till bed time; and then, dear Miss Bellasis, I'll come and sleep with you; and in order that you do neither yourself nor anybody else any harm, we'll first pop a nice little straight jacket over your chemise. It's not a very alarming garment. It's only a Garibaldi with the sleeves tied together."

There was clearly no help for Miss Bellasis.

"No habo remedis."

Dorothy came as announced by Miss Cope, and at ten o'clock that agreeable personage herself reappeared, to become Miss Bellasis's bedfellow.

She regaled her unfortunate companion while undressing with choice anecdotes of girls she had known who had been reclaimed from habits of untruthfullness and dishonesty by means of the birch.

"You'll be quite another girl after your flogging, Kate," she said, with affected geniality, as she slipped the Garibaldi which had been converted into a straight waistcoat over the head of the now unresisting prisoner.

Miss Cope slept soundly with the literally handcuffed girl by her side.

Kate's slumbers were broke and fitful; and a dozen times in her dreams did she see Miss Sinclair standing over her with the birch. But she did not feel it. O, dear, no.

Mrs. Rumble was up with the lark the next morning, to look after her much-cherished rods. She took them out of the brine, and found that the buds with which the twigs were plentifully bedecked, had swollen considerably under the action of the mingled marinade of salt, soda, and vinegar.

By the way if Charles Cotton's "Virgil travestie" is to be believed, it was once usual to soak rods in urine, or "in piss," as Mr. Cotton elegantly expresses it.

At present it is rare even that brine is used. What may be the practice in prisons or reformatories I know not; but I don't think that the Eton or Westminster boys are flogged with pickled rods.

Most notably pickled, however, were the rods prepared by Miss Sinclair's housekeeper for the bum of Miss Bellasis. She partially dried them, and then laid them out in state on one of the young ladies' drawing boards, where they lay bristling in labyrinthine twigginess, an alarming sight to view.

Breakfast, as usual, took place at eight o'clock. The meal was dispatched in dead silence. Half-an-hour's recreation followed, and at nine o'clock the entire school—with the exception, of course, of Miss Bellasis, were ranged in the long schoolroom, which was, in fact, an extension of the back parlour, and was built some forty or fifty feet into the playground.

This apartment made either one large schoolroom, or three separate ones; that is to say, it was divisible by wooden screens, sliding in frames, into three compartments, in which, upon occasion, as many classes could be carried on simultaneously without interfering with each other.

On the present occasion the barriers were open, and forty nine young ladies were in full view of Miss Sinclair, who was seated at her desk, or throne on a dais at the upper end.

The schoolmistress was very pale, and her countenance wore an expression of inexorable sternness, but she looked, nevertheless, marvellously handsome. The teachers, Miss Everard, Mlle. de la Tourelle, and Fraulein Schrobbs, did not occupy their usual posts, but stood in a group behind her.

Miss Sinclair rose:

"The following young ladies," she began, in a clear but hard voice, "will, as I name them, leave the room, repair to the dining room, and not presume to stir thence without my permission."

She named in quick succession about twenty-seven of the girls who were below the age of fourteen, and, as these damsels filed out of the schoolroom, in more than one countenance was an expression of intense disappointment visible.

Lucy Summerfield and Miriam Talbot, with Miss Haseltine, Miss Hatherton, and Marian Escott were among those permitted to remain.

As the last of the excluded list passed out, Miss Montis, the innocent fount and origin of all these evils, rose from her seat, went up to Miss Sinclair and addressed her in a low voice. She spoke English well enough, for she had been to school in Philadelphia before coming to England.

"I know what going to happen, dear Miss Sinclair," she said. "You give Miss Bellasis the flog-whip, eh. I not say she not merit it. But the flog-whip not a sight for a Castilian young lady to see. If I have a bad slave, I send her away to be flog. Let me go away, and not see Miss Kitty have the whip."

"As you please," answered the schoolmistress.

The lazy, good-natured Montis yawned, threw a glance, half of curiosity, half of contempt, on the little knot of governesses, and sauntered out of the room.

The schoolmistress now caused the lowest of the three screens to be pulled down, so that the schoolroom was divided into two, the upper being double the size of the inferior portion.

On the forms of this upper room the twenty-two elder girls were commanded to seat themselves, which they did in dead silence.

Before Miss Sinclair's desk a considerable open space was left.

"Now, Miss Everard," said the schoolmistress, when the young ladies were all seated, "perhaps you will be good enough to have Miss Bellasis brought here."

The head governess rang the schoolroom bell. The signal was evidently expected, and understood above, for in the course of about two minutes the prisoner of the Red Room was marched in between Miss Cope and Mrs. Rumble.

The housekeeper was not quite so ill-natured as Miss Cope, and although she had little pity for the condemned culprit, felt just that amount of human interest in her that a sergeant of marines might do who administered a dose of rum and gunpowder on the sly to a poor devil who was about to be brought up to the gangway.

Thus, when Mrs. Rumble went to call Miss Bellasis and tell her that she was "wanted below," she brought her a cup of hot tea, which was very grateful to the prisoner, who had had nothing but bread and water since the previous day.

"What have you put in it," whispered Miss Cope, observing that Kate paused in swallowing the fluid. "Nearly half-a-quartern of brandy," replied the housekeeper. "She'd be able to bear it better."

"Hum!" said Miss Cope, "it will enable her, perhaps, to bear more. I'll tell Miss Sinclair she's had brandy and she'll lay it on harder."

Kate Bellasis then entered the schoolroom, and stood up in custody before Miss Sinclair's desk. The girl was paler than her mistress—ashy white, indeed—only the spirit in the tea had brought out, on each cheek, a slight hectic spot.

She was dressed in a plain black silk dress, made tight to the shape, and fastening at the throat.

Those were the days of crinoline, and Miss Cope had maliciously recommended Miss Bellasis to dispense with that article of attire that morning.

"You'll only have to take it off again," she said, with a sneer.

Miss Bellasis had followed her advice.

The schoolmistress looked at her from head to foot with superb disdain. She stepped down from her desk, confronted the prisoner, almost putting her face in hers—then turned from her with an expression of disgust.

"Have you anything to say?" she asked.

"No, Madam, save that I was mad."

"So you told Miss Cope yesterday. We have physic here to cure mad people. You will be very sane at the end of half-an-hour. Have you anything more to say?"

"Forgive me, Miss Sinclair; I am sure that my

papa—"

As she faltered out these words Kate's eyes were anxiously travelling round in quest of the rod. She did not see any implement of chastisement, and a spark of hope was kindled in her bosom. Perhaps, after all, Miss Sinclair would only give her a severe lecture, and forgive her. But the spark was soon trampled out.

"Your papa," returned the schoolmistress, "will, I hope, be very grateful to me for the course I am about to adopt with his daughter. It is better, after all, that only her schoolfellows should witness her disgrace, than that she should be given in charge to a policeman, and dragged handcuffed through the streets of Brighton to the station-house. I have but to lift my little finger—I have but to utter a word—and such would be your fate. You have committed an act of felony, punishable by a long term of imprisonment, if not of penal servitude. Respect for your father's position deters me from giving you over to the law for punishment. It is not through any tenderness for you that I forego prosecution. As much shame and as much pain as I can make you suffer you shall endure between these four walls. Do you hear me? Shame and pain. In another moment you will be made acquainted with the sight of a birch rod, if you have never seen one before—(Miss Sinclair, herself, had never seen one in her life)—the stripes of that rod will give you pain, suffering, and anguish more terrible than you ever felt in your life. But that is not all. Shame must be added. Shame in the knowledge that you, a young lady of position—you, whose papa and mamma keep their carriage—you, a grown-up girl, who in another year will be presented at the Court of your Sovereign—you, who think yourself pretty, and witty, and clever, have been scourged as the child is scourged—as female thieves and wantons used to be scourged—that you have been exposed naked and bound before your schoolfellows. Liar and thief—your hour is come. You are about to be flogged."

Miss Bellasis sank on her knees, her eyes streaming with tears.

"For God's sake spare me, Madam," she cried.

"Not one lash of your flogging will I spare you; and don't take the Almighty's name in vain, you wicked girl, or I'll have you gagged."

"Miss Sinclair, forgive me, I implore you."

"Oh, yes; I dare say. 'I will be good; I will be good: I'll never do so any more.' Perhaps you'll tell me that, next. Mrs. Rumble, fetch the rods."

The housekeeper left the room.

"Now," resumed the schoolmistress, to the still kneeling Kate, "be good enough to get up, Miss, or I'll cane you till you do."

And to the general surprise Miss Sinclair produced from the back of her desk a long little cane—it was the one with which she had begun to whip Lucy Summerfield—and struck Miss Bellasis across the shoulders.

The production of this cane was not entirely of Miss Sinclair's inspiration. She had received very early that morning a little note from Mr. Calvedon, in which Arthur, after repeating that he would be at Verbena House by noon, added—

"You will find a light cane or switch very useful while the young lady is getting ready, and in the event of her proving refractory; but be careful and use it over her clothes."

Miss Bellasis sprang to her feet with an exclamation more of anger than of pain, when she felt, for the first time, the infliction of a cane.

"How dare you?" she said, almost beside herself.

"How dare I? How dare I? How dare I?" echoed Miss

Sinclair, accompanying each interrogatory with a fresh blow of the cane across the girl's back and shoulders.

"That's how I dare. Hold out your hand this moment?"

"I will not," cried Kate, stamping her foot.

"Miss Cope," said the schoolmistress, simply.

Miss Cope knew her business. She stepped forward and seized Kate by the right arm, just above the wrist, and held out the girl's hand horizontally. She obstinately closed her fist, and a shower of stripes descended on her knuckles. She writhed and twisted like an eel under the agony, biting her lips till the blood came, and at last, in sheer exhaustion, opened her hand.

Miss Sinclair gave her six stripes with all her strength.

"Now the other hand."

Seemingly cowed, Miss Bellasis excented her similar palm, and received six more cuts, wincing and shuddering, but uttering no cry.

She had really received what in ordinary schools might me termed "a good caning," but Miss Sinclair's appetite for punishment was, as yet, barely awakened.

She laid the cane down on the desk; took breath; sat down even, eyeing the culprit with eyes almost gloating in their intensity of survey.

But soon another—and more exciting—object claimed her attention.

Mrs. Rumble marched up the schoolroom, bearing the moist and budding birches on the drawing-board, as solemnly as though she were Herodias carrying the head of John the Baptist on a charger.

The bosom of the schoolmistress heaved when she saw these great, branching rods, brown and sharp, and shining from their recent bath of brine. Her fingers quivered to clutch the scourges. The blood raced through her veins; her backbone seemed to open and shut; the saliva gathered on her tongue; and her breath seemed to her hot as a furnace blast. She put her hand to her head, and the veins of her temples were throbbing, and her hair was wet.

"Oh!" she thought, "If Arthur could only be here. If it were only twelve o'clock."

As for Miss Bellasis, she contemplated the birch with an aspect of stark, haggard horror.

She had heard of such a thing; read of it in novels; heard her brothers from Eton joke about it; had joked about it herself with other girls; but here was the actual, horrible thing, itself, more frightful, more appalling, than ever she could have imagined it to be.

No wretch condemned to be hanged ever eyed the gallows and the drop with more heart-sickening affright than Kate Bellasis looked upon the birch.

Mrs. Rumble laid these dread paraphernalia on the desk, and, folding her hands before her, awaited further orders.

"Ready?" Miss Sinclair whispered to her.

"Quite ready, ma'am."

"Strip!" cried the schoolmistress, to Miss Bellasis.

The unhappy girl had taken a sudden, desperate, resolution.

"I will not. Miss Sinclair, it is a scandal, a shame—I am grown up; I am a young woman."

"If you were five-and-twenty years of age you should be flogged, and stripped to receive your flogging. Off with your clothes I say."

"I'll scream, I'll write to my papa."

"You may scream the house down, and no attention will be paid to your cries. The servants know that you are going to be birched for thieving, the lady next door knows it. As for writing to your papa, I'll give you pens, ink and paper, and a postage stamp to write to Mr.

Bellasis—after you have been soundly flogged. Stay; you don't want a postage stamp. You are a grown up young lady; you have ten shillings a week pocket money."

This was said sarcastical, as Artemus Ward used to say, and was received with a titter of appreciation by the knot of governesses.

The girls were too much absorbed by the tragic interest of the scene to laugh.

Miss Bellasis folded her arms, and repeated, "I will not. I will die first."

"You will be birched before you die," observed Miss Sinclair, cooly; "meanwhile we must make you do what you might do yourself. Miss Everard, Miss Cope, Mrs. Rumble, undress her."

The head governess, the under-teacher, and the housekeeper advanced, and, in sensational language, "seized their prey."

But Mrs. Rumble was a wary woman, and accustomed to deal with refractory subjects. While Miss Everard and Miss Cope held Kate fast by the arms, the housekeeper very quietly pushed her knee against the girl's back. Kate tottered, and in another moment she was comfortable seated on the floor, while Mrs. Rumble was dexterously unlacing her boots.

"You oughtn't to have let her put'em on, Miss," she said to Miss Cope. "With those high heels she'd a kicked us awful. Now, my darling," she continued, looking at the poor prostrate daughter of the "Q.C.," "you may kick your feet off, if you like."

By this time the two governesses had pulled off Miss Bellasis's dress, and undone her petticoat strings; they then raised her to her feet, and dragging down the mass of linen and flannel drapery made her step out of it. There was some difficulty in unlacing her stays, but a sharp penknife, handed to Miss Everard by the schoolmistress, soon settled that difficulty.

"What on earth did you let her lace herself up so tight for, Miss Cope," whispered the housekeeper. "She didn't want no stays, poor thing. You might have brought her down in her nightgown."

"I'm sure I acted for the best," exclaimed the under-teacher, pettishly. "I told her not to put on her crinoline; but I let her have her stays because I thought Miss Sinclair might only pull up her clothes. At all events, they're off now."

Yes; they were off, and pitiably had the girl screamed—desperately had she struggled during the ignominious operation. But what could she do against three strong women, with three more standing by, and ready to lend assistance if required. Nay, I think that more than one of the elder girls would have willingly assisted in divesting Miss Bellasis of her raiment.

Her hair had become loosened during the conflict, and was streaming down her back. The net which confined it—nets were worn in those days—was torn to shreds.

Miss Cope was good enough to take off her own net, and as she crammed Miss Bellasis's golden tresses into the bag, she couldn't help muttering to herself, "I should like to cut off her hair, I should, the minx."

The tormentors released their hold on this poor "minx" for a moment. You might have thought them so many cats giving delusive "law" to a mouse.

Surely Kate Bellasis must have been mad; for, mouse-like she profited by her momentary enlargement to endeavour to escape.

The cruel girls burst into a shout of laughter as they saw the belle of the school in her shift rush down the schoolroom towards the door.

The career of this new Atalanta was suddenly arrested; for, behind the door, when she opened it, she found the cook, the housemaid, and the boy Stiggles, who had all been greedily watching the preliminaries of execution.

By this time Miss Sinclair, who, motioning to her subordinates to keep their places, had hurried, cane in hand, after the fugitive, rushed into the lobby, caught Kate by the right arm, and dragged her into the schoolroom again.

Beckoning to Miss Everard and Miss Cope, she gave the captured runaway into their custody, and then returned to the lobby.

The domestics were scurrying away when she recalled them.

"As you have seen so much," she said, smiling, "you may as well see the rest. Only, keep the door ajar. You, too, Master Stiggles, may remain. I shall have something to say to you afterwards."

The schoolmistress then returned to her desk. Her fingers itched to lay the cane once more over Miss Bellasis's back; but she desisted and reserved all her energies for the birch.

"Up with her on the desk, ladies," she cried.

Miss Bellasis was now undressed with the exception of her chemise, drawers, and stockings, and an under-chemise of silk.

The women dragged her to Miss Sinclair's desk, which had been turned round so that the sloping part on which the culprit was to be laid should be in full view of the audience. Mrs. Rumble had brought down a couple of pillows from the bedrooms, and these she first proceeded to lay upon the desk in order that they might afford a cushion for the sufferer.

These delicate attentions, when you are going to flog anybody till the blood comes, are very touching. A soldier tied up to the halberds, or to the triangle has a stool to lean against. Some flogging-blocks in boys' schools are stuffed like chairs, and the heels and loins even of garrotters are in some prisons protected by coils of wadding before punishment commences.

Miss Bellasis was "hitched up," so to speak, till her navel was about over the desk flap. Her belly was well buried in a pillow, and on another she laid her face. She could just see over the desk. As to her legs they were about a foot from the ground.

Miss Sinclair was at first about to place a stool beneath her knees; but, on reflection, it struck her that she would be more helpless with her legs pendant. In fact, under the last-named circumstances, she would be the facto "horsed."

Acting under the schoolmistress' directions, Miss Cope tied the girl's legs together with some soft silken window cord.

Mrs. Rumble took a firm grasp of one of the girl's arms and Mademoiselle De la Tourelle of the other; while with another length of silken cord her hands were tied together at the wrists.

Fraulein Schrobbs was given to understand that her particular department was to hold the sufferer's drapery up.

The services of Miss Everard were needed as an active agent.

When these preparations were complete, a happy thought struck Miss Everard. Kate's legs were certainly tied together, but she might still lift them, and give a conjoint kick to the person operating on her backside.

At first Miss Sinclair thought of calling one of the housemaids to hold her legs; but the bright idea which occurred to her was to attach one end of the cord to a heavy weight—one of some thirty pounds, perhaps—which was used for keeping the door open when needed.

"She won't kick that up," thought Miss Sinclair. All was now in readiness. The three birches had been removed to a chair by the side of the desk.

"Pull up her chemise," cried Miss Sinclair, to Fraulein Schrobbs. The German governess raised the shift, not without difficulty, for the last convulsive act of Kate when she was laid on the desk was to stuff the front of the garment between her thighs. However it was dragged up by the Fraulein, and laid in folds over the small of her back.

"Now her drawers; pull down her drawers," said Miss Sinclair.

"Oh! let me keep my drawers on? do let me keep my drawers on?" pleaded the culprit, who had evidently abandoned resistance as useless.

"Let me be punished on the back, dear Miss Sinclair—not down there, it's so disgraceful."

"I know it is," returned the schoolmistress grimly, "that is why I am going to flog you there. Down with them, Fraulein Schrobbs.

Thus adjured the Teutonic instructress undid the string of Miss Bellasis's pantaloons, which were of the finest linen, richly laced round the hems, and drew them down over the calves of her legs. But here a slight disappointment awaited Miss Sinclair. Nay, more than a mere disappointment, almost a feeling of agony; a terrible, creeping, crawling fear that the wished-for flogging would have to be put off.

What; grant a respite? Never! And yet she must, for Miss Bellasis, with her tender drawers softly clinging to her ankles, had not even by this time disclosed the whole expanse of her naked bum. There was an obstacle in the way, and that was nothing more than a piece of linen, in shape like those horsehair bands that we men rub our shoulders with after our morning tubs. It was wider in the middle than at the ends. It was placed between her legs, one end being brought up in front and the other behind; in short it was a "periodical" cloth—a bandage for the "monthlies."

"Miss Sinclair's fear now died away as rapidly as it had come. She remembered that Miss Bellasis had "smashed her tomatoes," as the French say, but eight days since. She breathed again, and the moisture that had been drying up between her thighs and getting gummy, oozed out once more, thicker and warmer than ever.

There was no doubt about it. Miss Sinclair was rapidly becoming a real lady flagellant. She enjoyed in anticipation the coming punishment, she thirsted for it, she wanted it; she must flog, she must cut up a bottom! She was doomed to excoriate bums, to weal posteriors for the remaining term of her life. The letch had got as tight hold of her as it has of me, I who have mangled backsides all over the world, although there is nothing like the hard buttocks of a fair English lass.

The French woman has generally a knowledge of all letches, and being selfish and mercenary, wants to be paid in consequence. Money and "minette," those are the two talismans that point the way to the heart of the Parisienne.

Spanish maidens are too fiery-tempered to submit easily, and besides that, their bottoms are too tough and brown and wiry.

As we go south bottoms decrease and bubbies expand. Give me the posteriors of the north. I shall never forget a lovely St. Petrsburg wench I castigated once. She was tall and fair, even to the whitey-brown state. She was all over Russian embroidery, red and blue above, but underneath she was dirty. When I lifted her petticoats there was a very pronounced "odor di femina," like stale shrimps. I did not mind that, only I could not succeed in hurting her much. I slapped and slapped, not a birch being handy, but I only made my hand ache. So I took my brache and cut into her with the ends. The buckles raised blisters, but she took it manfully. There are used to being whacked in the land of the knout.

"Remove that rag! Take away that base bandage," she was going to say "bauble," like Oliver Cromwell. But she restrained herself in time, so as not to make herself ridiculous before her open-mouthed pupils.

Poor Miss Sinclair! Her bosom was heaving, her eyes felt hot. She was in a fever of lust.

She continued her voice slightly hoarse:

"It is perfectly useless to pretend indisposition, as I know from Mrs. Rumble, that she passed through her monthly sexual derangement about a week since."

No sooner were the words out of her mouth than Fraulein Schrobbs began to fumble with the rag, but Mdlle. de la Tourelle darted quickly forward, and tore it away. These Gallic natures are very quick and lively.

"Voila!" she squeaked out as she triumphantly flourished it over her head, like a flag, "il n'y a rien!"

And there was indeed nothing to be seen, not a stain. At last the bottom of the Bellasis was really exposed to view. It was a real perfect posterior. It swelled out grandly, properly, and gradually from a sloping small of the back that would have satisfied a Grecian sculptor. There were two lovely dimples just above the top and below a couple of sharply-defined creases, caused by the over powering swelling of the hemispheres, now that the thighs were tightly pressed together. This pressure caused the lovely mountains to crease up all over. They showed health by their hardness, and terror by the goose-flesh look they had, reminding one of a smooth lake rippled by the summer breeze. It was a regal bum, and yet tough withal. One that would take a fair amount of punishment, for this was the skin of a brunette, akin to the Spanish ones I mentioned just now. It combined the rich golden hue of the beauties of the sunny land, with the firmness inherent to all the well-nourished, beefy backsides of our tight little island.

The victim had shut her eyes, clenched her hands, and her livid lips were tightened together. She was ready.

The pupils were not at their ease. One had evidently forgotten herself, and her comrades shrank from her. She had uncorked her scent bottle, or, in other words, the unusual trepidation had acted on her bowels, and the disturbed gases were slowly escaping. The others mostly felt as if "they had something going up and down inside them." So they described their sensations to each other in thick whispers, all their saliva being dried up long since.

Miss Sinclair, her fine figure drawn up to its full height, as red as a turkey cock, poses the rod in a nervously-tightened grasp, calculates the distance; and whistling through the air the supple bunch of twigs comes firmly down across the flesh, immediately leaving a long red mark behind it. A long suppressed groan came from the lips of the lady thief; but she clenched her teeth, and only just in time as the second cut came surely slanting across both cheeks. It was a smarting cut indeed; so much so that a piece of twig flew to the ceiling, which plainly shows that rods cannot be too well pickled. Miss Sinclair fairly enjoyed it. She stood as firm as a rock, and cut after cut, blow after blow, was inflicted in rapid succession. Her mouth watered.

Miss Bellasis had now given up all idea of resistance; she shrieks out pitifully, "Not so hard! not so hard! Ah! ah! No! no! Don't, don't; pray don't."

Pitiless the birch came regularly down, working like

the Nasmyth steam hammer. There was no deviating from the proper spot, no useless feeble blows; no striking of the thighs nor of the small of the back, nothing but ruthless idea to murder those splendid posteriors. They were beginning to change colour. First they started into two large red spots that covered the whole surface of the "fesses."

Then the redness grew darkened, and formed strange, blackish-violet ridges and waves.

The girl's eyes filled with tears, and a bright vivid line of carmine appeared on her lips. Her nervous clenching of the teeth had caused the blood to start from her gums.

"You bad girl!" hissed Miss Sinclair; "see, see, see"— and she punctuated each word with a murderous stroke of the terrible rod—"see what your wicked instincts have brought upon you." Miss Bellasis writhed under an unusually wicked blow, and stretched her buttocks still more asunder, as she tried to get away from the punishment, and forced her belly further against the desk, as if to crush her body into it.

"Mercy, do have mercy!"

"No mercy for the thief!"

"I did not know what I was doing. I—oh! pity! pity!"

"Your tears affect me not, you idle, vicious hussy. You rob your fellow scholars, do you? You'll rob your parents next, and finish on the gallows, you vile girl."

The dividing line of the two globes now appeared strangely white in comparison with the other swollen and inflamed parts. She was stretching and grinding her body about all ways to get relief. Her executioner's eyes glistened as she noticed this, and getting more in front of her, so as to gloat over the massacred bottom, she threw away the rod, now worn to a useless stump.

Miss Bellasis thought it was over, and so did her

affrighted schoolmates, a sigh of relief issuing from their lips.

The tears swelled up from the eyes of the tightly-bound victim.

"Let me go now, and I will never offend any more."

"You should have reflected beforehand," said her inflexible schoolmistress. "I have not done yet. I'll make you smart. You shall never forget this chastisement as long as you live."

Catherine groaned and shut her eyes. The Fraulein slightly hysterical and not knowing whether to laugh or to cry, rolled up the girl's chemise, and carefully adjusted it out of the way of the rod.

The French girl stood looking on with her eyes starting out of her head, and two hectic flushes on her cheeks, while her fingers were working as if she would like to hold a rod herself. The sight of the distended, bruised buttocks had simply caused a violent erection of a horny clitoris, followed by a copious emission.

In the doorway was a remarkable group. There was Dorothy and the cook, both with hot faces and eager eyes. The fat queen of the kitchen was leaning on her companion, and behind them, his goblin face leering between the two, was that boy Stiggles. One hand was up Dolly's clothes, and with the other he was rubbing his foreskin backwards and forwards. Nay, why disguise the fact? the young b——r was f——g himself. His right hand had pinched her calves.

She twisted and tried to evade his touch, but was too frightened to make much disturbance in the matter, for fear of being ordered away. So his hand crept on and felt her knees. They were rounded and well covered, but slightly hard from having often knelt so scrub the floors and hearthstone doorsteps. His grubby fingers nicely warmed, crept up the sturdy thighs, and then invaded the bouquet of mossy hair that hid her crack, sufficiently nourished with respectable layers of adipose tissue.

She starts and pinches her legs lightly together, but the erotic effect began to make itself manifest. What with the spectacle of Miss Sinclair hard at work on the girl's bum, and the pushing energy of Stiggles's satyr-like and perspiring hand, she gave way gently, and the broad finger of the lad soon found itself encased in a hot moist receptacle.

Here his touch began to get furious, and being in real earnest, he soon brought down gentle gushes of her warm creamy essence. He made her come more than once, f——g her with her own slimy liquid, and rubbing his small and hard member quickly and slowly, keeping time to the swish, swish of the tickle-toby.

Let us leave these menial masturbators to their engrossing pleasures, and hie back to our heroine.

Miss Everard, holding the second rod in her hand, had enjoyed the punishment as much as anybody, standing near Miss Sinclair, with whom she was a special favourite.

"Miss Everard," said Miss Sinclair, "I am satisfied—I may say, disgusted at this work, so unusual for me. I beg you will take my place. Continue."

A ferocious smile of pleasure lit up the teacher's face as she stepped forward, rod in hand.

"No! no! Not you—you have no right. Oh! do; do let me go now. It burns and cuts so awfully," sobbed out the victim.

"Silence, thief!" said the mistress of Verbena House, and turning to Miss Everard, who was awaiting further orders, said "let her have it."

Nothing loath, the new rod was soon set agoing. Miss Everard, held it tightly, and whisked it down with fearful force, making great use of the ends. The skin was now extended to bursting, and the swollen black weals and blisters were beginning to break. The white untouched furrow between the two tortured hills seemed to tempt this second flagellation, and she went at it till she had brought it to the same colour as the rest of the bottom.

Miss Sinclair began to lecture, having got her wind by this time.

"All your schoolfellows have now thoroughly seen the shame and disgrace that one bad action can bring upon a girl, who obstinately refusing to profit by the daily lessons of good I try to inculcate, will not learn to distinguish between the laws of meum and tuum, and appropriated to herself the property of others. The devil shall be driven out of you, and, in future, any of my young lady pupils who, undeterred by this dreadful example, may follow in your footsteps and become criminals, shall meet with the same fate. Miss Everard, a little harder, please."

Miss Bellasis, it is very probable, heard but little of the speech, being engaged in shrieking as loudly as she could. And no wonder, for the Everard fiend needed but very little telling to strike home. She sent the birch hissing through the air, cutting recklessly into bottom and thighs. These white columns were being pickled now. Miss Everard liked to lay it on the fresh places.

The cries of Miss Bellasis were awful, as she twisted, and writhed, and wriggled about, but all in vain.

Her "ah's," "don't's," "not so hard," "not there" (as the thighs came in for their share), &c., were unheeded, and the second rod was worn to a stump, Miss Everard's arm aching from the wrist to the shoulder.

"Ah! ah!! ah!!! Great heavens! Have mercy! I can't bear it! I can't! I can't!" she screamed, struggling so furiously that it required all the force of Schrobbs and La Tourelle to hold her in a proper position.

Miss Sinclair was now as pale as death, from flushed as she was before.

"Beware of my rod, now that I have learned to use it, ladies all."

And she took up the third fatal bunch of twigs.

There was a terrible hush, as all knew this was to be the last act of the terrible drama of correction.

"How do you like it, Miss Bellasis? Tell your schoolmates how nice it is;" and she slowly and deliberately lashed at the scarified posterior that presented a piteous sight.

"Ah—r—r—e! Ah! oh! I shall expire if you don't forgive me, dear Miss Sinclair. I am, indeed, shockingly punished. It's red hot!"

Miss Sinclair's innate desire at present, although she would hardly have dared to confess it to herself, was to draw her victim's blood. Heedless of the low sobs, groans, moans, and hysterical crying of the poor girl, she cut at the parts that presented the most weals, and soon from the capricious arabesques a slow stream of blackened sanguineous fluid began to issue gently forth. This heightened her wrath; she "saw red," and, lashing away with the greatest fury, the once lovely buttocks became a hideous mass of raw, gory flesh; the blood, which had got red and bright, flowing freely, even trickling down to the tops of the offender's stockings, which soon became spotted and stained.

"Will you do so again? Will you rob, and thieve, and pilfer, and steal again?"

Each question was accentuated by a more terrific cut, as pieces of birch flew in all directions.

Miss Bellasis could only groan out a faint. "No! no! Never again, I promise!" and she fainted away as Miss Sinclair let the shattered remnants of the last rod drop from her hand.

Immediately there was a revolution of feeling, and all the bystanders, who had thoroughly enjoyed the whipping, did their utmost to succour the object of their amusement.

She was soon untied, and her bottom, which was simply flayed of every particle of skin, carefully hidden, while she was quickly born away to bed.

Everybody was seemingly satisfied that justice had been done. The floor was strewed with pieces of rod, and Miss Sinclair had very nearly spent, but she was not wholly pleased yet. Her blood was on fire, as she staggered to her private parlour, with one regret filling her mind—she had not seen Miss Bellasis's c—t!

She thought of this now it was too late, and the rage she felt at this omission demanded more scourging of other girls, so that she might see how the sexual parts in front appeared, when the corresponding regions behind were being cruelly and brutally entreated.

The demon of the rod had got Miss Sinclair, of Verbena House, tight into his clutches, and her parched lips seemed to say—"More birch! More birch!"

Dorothy had never been in such a state of luscious excitement in her life. She had lost all count of the number of times Stiggles had f——d her to an emission. He also had rubbed himself till he could rub no more, and had ejaculated into the back of the housemaid's print gown, which was sticky with his youthful tribute, the pendant apron strings behind dripping with the white and viscous fluid.

As for the girls they really did not know whether they were on their heads or their unfledged tails, nor what on earth was the matter with them.

They rushed to the playground, and formed there into excited groups, when the conversation turned upon the horrors of the sight they had just witnessed, drifting off awhile into smutty talk of what had occurred during the last holidays, and at Christmas parties.

Miss Waterhouse had never seen a man's affair, so Miss Talbot described a large specimen she had got a glimpse of when on a visit to Paris. A Frenchman, using one of those open urinals that line the Boulevards, had turned round as the English miss passed, and had playfully shaken his virile member at her.

Miss Clayton had sat upon her uncle's lap, and felt him get hard as she moved about on the Priapus that grew up between her thighs; while Miss Moleskin had actually let her first cousin, Ernest Doodledash, who was at school with the Jesuits, feel her sprouting bubbies several times during a children's ball.

The indolent Creole sat apart while this conversation was going on. She, like the young waterman of lyric fame, "was thinking of nothing at all," as she sat, with eyes half closed, scratching her head and picking her nose with great gusto, basking the while in the sun like a dirty Italian fisherman's whore of Naples.

Miss Sinclair entered her private parlour, threw herself into an arm chair, shut her eyes, and breathed heavily.

The blinds were half down, the curtains were nearly drawn, and a cool quiet demi-jour pervaded the cosy snuggery.

She was all to pieces, her hand ached—the hand that had clutched the rod; her bosom had started and worked itself out of her stays; there was a gentle perspiration on her noble forehead, and, to tell the truth in the plainest of English, she felt awfully randy.

She panted fitfully as she reclined with her legs apart, letting the inflamed parts cool themselves as best they might. Her tongue uneasily licked her parched lips as she murmured to herself the bawdiest words she could think of—"fuck! fuck!" she gently whispered; and then she murmured, "prick, prick; cunt, cunt."

Her hand stole then slyly to her slit. She caressed herself, and moistening her fingers at the entrance to the vagina, rubbed her damp digits over a fat, crisp, and robust clitoris.

The friction seemed to bring her to; she sighed, shuddered, and opened her eyes.

At last she seemed to be conscious of what she was about; she blushed, although alone, put down her clothes, and, standing up, stood in front of the chimney-glass, smoothed her hair and dabbed her face with a handkerchief redolent with the cheap perfume that Schweitzer, of the King's-road, sells to the little milliners, who often get half-a-sovereign on summer nights for frigging old gentlemen on the beach, underneath the pier.

From the horrors that her chaste lips have dropped during her solitary reflections, it may be easily seen that the proprietor of Verbena House was not a virgin.

She was an unfortunate spinster, who had been heartily fucked when young, but had always hidden her irregularities under a cloak of outward respectability. Now that she was advancing in age, and that the epoch for the cessation of her menstrual flux was nigh in a few years, she turned once more in imagination to the delights of love, and all through Miss Bellasis's beautiful bum.

At this moment there was a gentle rap at the door.

"Who is there?" said Miss Sinclair, turning round.

The voice of the housemaid Dorothy replied.

"Please, ma'am, it's the Reverend Mr. Calvedon."

Miss Sinclair started, looked once more in the glass, smiled to herself, bit her lips to make them appear red, and advancing quickly towards the door, opened it in an instant.

The Rev. Arthur, clean shaven, and as neat as a new pin, was on Dorothy's heels. The housemaid gave way, and the High Church lady's darling was soon over the mat.

The door closed. He seized both Miss Sinclair's hands, and pressed them in his own.

"Well, my dear Miss Sinclair?" and he paused mischievously.

Miss Sinclair sank on to the end of a well-stuffed sofa. Arthur seated himself in front of her on a low chair, still holding her moist palms in his cool grasp.

"Don't ask me. Really, I do not know whether I am on my head or my heels. The punishment to which I was forced to subject that bad, wilful girl, has acted upon my nervous system in such a fearful manner. I shall never recover the shock."

Arthur could see how her bosom was heaving; how her eyes sparkled, and he began to think there was a chance to get her into his lecherous clutches. Now when a man makes up his mind to his, and, above all, a smooth-tongued, sturdy rogue of a priest, the female has no more chance than a mouse with a cat.

"My poor lady," he murmured, with the golden voice that so gently used to soothe his female penitents at the church leading out of West-street. "My worldly experience is but scant, but I think I can very nearly guess the tumultuous feelings that sway your tender heart."

He here let go her unresisting hands, put one knee close to hers, and laid his right hand, which was white, carefully tended, and loaded with rings, on her thigh.

It was Tartuffe over again.

"I remember once that on the complaint of a severe parent, who had given his son into my charge to prepare him for an examination, I resolved to subject the stubborn youth of sixteen to a slight course of severe castigation."

Here he paused to watch the effect of his story on Miss Sinclair. She was listening attentively, so he got up, and without saying a word, crossed to the door, turned the key, and returned to his seat.

"What are you doing, Mr. Calvedon?"

"I do not want to be disturbed, my dear lady, while I talk to you about correction inflicted this morning. Remember, that this is a very serious subject, as it may influence your whole system of education, which up to the present has been safely conducted without resorting to corporal punishment."

"Exactly so, my dear Sir; how you understand me," and she sighed heavily.

Arthur came a little nearer. I should think I did, he thought to himself; you are ripe for a fair honest rack-off, and so am I. I haven't had a poke for a fortnight, and you, my buxom wielder of the rod, I swear shall receive the whole lot, to the very last drop.

"To resume my story," continued he aloud, "I led the young man to my bedroom, and ordered him to let down his trousers and drawers, I fastened his hands with a rug-strap, pitched him forward on to the bed, and holding him down with one hand I cut at his lazy b——," and he stopped, coughed, and went on. Miss Sinclair making no sign, "with a hair brush, till he howled for mercy."

Miss Sinclair wriggled about uneasily, and then said:

"I do not quite see the analogy between my grief to-day at being forced against my nature to become cruel and almost bloodthirsty, if I may venture to say so, and your severity with your pupil."

Arthur grew impatient as he saw that his prey did not "rise" at his flagellating experiences, so he drew his chair nearer in, fastened his legs well against hers, caught hold of her hand, and went on quickly, unheeding her observation, his voice growing thick with emotion, and a neat lump of delight showing itself gradually on the left thigh of his sleek black pants.

"From that day, madam, I felt a strange pleasure in administering condign punishment to infants of either sex, and even adults sometimes became my victims. I guess your peculiar position to-day. You, too, feel these remarkable inward movements of the mind, and poor, weak, charming creature, are unable to analyse them as I did. I rushed to the works of the holy fathers, and soon Sanchez and Meibomius, Lanjuinais and Adrianssen told me that I had mastered the mystery of flagellation."

Miss Sinclair, her eyes starting out of her head at her secret thoughts being thus divined, fluttered like a bird just caught by a serpent, and could only just murmur a faint:

"I—I—I—don't understand you!"

"Of course, beautiful creature, those barbarous-sounding names of mouldy wiseacres mean nothing to you, but I will soon teach you the divine pleasure of whipping or being whipped, associated with the adorable delights of love when two healthy hearts and bodies beat together in unison, and join in luscious love!"

He lost no time, but slipping on to his knees winding his arm round her massive waist, and looking up into her eyes, played his trump card by whispering that tuneful sentence that never misses its effect, even when we know it to be false, and only paid for: "I love you!"

"Oh! Mr. Calvedon, I pray you! Don't! You have no right to talk thus to me. How dare you? Take your hands away! I'll call! Oh; Arthur! Oh!"

Any imaginative reader could fill up the blanks left in the foregoing disjointed sentences, but as I do not want to leave anything untold, I will try to explain what drew these fitful remonstrances from the lips of the fair proprietress of Verbena House.

The Reverend Arthur had followed up his simple declaration by tipping the luxurious form of Miss Sinclair backwards on the sofa. The sudden fall threw her legs sprawling in the air, and he profited by her position to get between them, throwing up her clothes at the same time. It did not take the adroit rogue long to open her drawers wide, push away the tail of her chemise, and take a long look at the ripe cunt he had so often longed for.

It was as perfect an one as can readily be imagined. Pierced rather high, the top of the crack formed a soft cushion, well covered with black hair that grew luxuriously almost up to the navel. The emotion of the morning had slightly opened it, so that a glimpse of the interior could be seen of a rich, pale pink; the saucy clitoris, moist and red, looking as if the sly twat was putting its tongue out at you. There was none of those signs of chafing that are often discernable on the inner sides of mature ladies' thighs, but all was white and well tended. And there went up a sweet scent of under-linen that had been in lavender, mingled with that nameless faint marine perfume that we all enjoy.

Arthur's nostrils took in the rising breeze of the mellow crack, and his eyes enjoyed the sight of the sticky spendings that garnished the entrance to the grotto.

His fingers eagerly pressed the lips together, and a rapid friction of the slippery button of enjoyment soon made the lady clench her hands, hold her tongue, shut her eyes, and begin to enjoy it.

She felt that any more resistance on her part would only cause useless struggles.

She had all to loose and nothing to gain, unless she made up her mind to be well fucked. So she did so, and laid with her legs well open, one arm thrown across and hiding her face, intending to submit with enjoyment to all the lecherous vagaries of her priestly lover.

Arthur, still keeping his eyes upon the moist cunt, silk garters, and hose, well-made boots and frilled petticoats, undid his trousers, and slipping them over his heels, was soon in the proper position to storm the citadel.

He wore no drawers or braces, like an old rowing-man as he was, so tucking up his shirt under his vest, he disclosed his muscular thighs and strong calves, that proved he was "fit" and in good condition. His balls were very hard and full, and his thick prick was standing up, arched towards his belly, a pearl of preparatory sperm starting from the orifice of the urethra.

He took hold of his penis, leant forward, moved it rapidly up and down twice or thrice just within the lips, then heaved a sigh of enjoyment, and plunged the whole shaft right into the willing vagina letting go of it as he dashed on, till he touched her womb, and caused her to start from her recumbent position.

There was no show of prudery now; no more complaints; nothing but sighs and kisses, as Miss Sinclair responded to his embrace by throwing her arms around him, and heaving up to his furious strokes.

He clutched her still tighter, stifled her incoherent exclamations of delight by the simple process of thrusting his tongue as far between her teeth as he conveniently could, and giving a furious push that caused the sofa to groan and creak, exclaimed:

"Oh! my God! I must! I must!"

And with these words the accumulation of boiling extract of manhood inundated the innermost recesses of the rich, tight cunt that he had been so industriously plugging.

Miss Sinclair had already spent, but this discharge shooting properly close upon the entrance to her womb, brought down her love-juice again, and she shuddered with delight, turned up her eyes, and went off almost into a swoon, exclaiming:

"Oh! Arthur—Mr. Calvedon! Shake me—move me—or I shall faint!"

He withdrew his member, still partially erect, and taking her in his arms, undid the bosom of her dress, then her stays, and kissing her ear playfully and gently, bit the cartilage, which judicious treatment had the required effect, and soon brought her to.

"Oh! you bad man!" she said smilingly, as the Rev. Arthur was feeling her bubbies, which were large, not too flabby, and with two hard dark red nipples.

"I do like you! Oh! it was so nice! You'll always love me, won't you?"

Arthur was seated by her side, one arm round her waist, the other in her bosom.

"Love you, darling. Won't I? And how happy we shall be. I'll teach you such nice things, such loving ways of enjoyment. I'll kiss you all over, you beauty!"

And leaning forward, he licked her neck, under her chin, and descended to her breasts, which he fingered and sucked in turn. Then he separated them, and burying his face between, brought the pliable globes fast against his cheeks, still gently wagging his pointed tongue the while.

"Arthur, dear, don't; you make me feel so funny. Just the same as I was while beating Miss Bellasis."

"Of course," said Arthur, rising up, "there's nothing like beating backsides to make one feel inclined for lovers' sport. Would you believe, darling, that there are grown-up men who like to be whipped by their sweet ladies, and instead of it hurting them, they enjoy the punishment, and the girls get the best of it too, for they can do their duty much better afterwards."

"No; really, Arthur, is that true? How strange!"

"Look here, I'll show you."

And our impetuous clergyman threw himself on his stomach across her knees, and pulling up his shirt behind, disclosed to her astonished view his well-knit, hairy posterior.

"Now, dear, slap me with all your might and main. Go on!"

Miss Sinclair giggled, and making a slight movement as if to push him off her knees, said:

"How ridiculous! No; I never could, I'm certain."

"Do, darling, do," implored Arthur, wriggling about so as to push his prick about between her thighs, "and you'll see how nice it will be afterwards."

"You silly creature," said the amorous schoolmistress, who was really getting very fond of her Arthur, and she bent her head and kissed the cheeks of the manly bottom she had been secretly admiring.

"Now, then beauty, hit as hard as you can!"

Miss Sinclair caught him round the middle, laughed, and slapped him feebly, as she began to enjoy the rubbing of his prick, once more stiff and wiry.

"Your hand is so nice, dear, but you don't hit hard enough," sighed Arthur.

"Is that better?" she said, as the old "Bellasis feeling" came over her at the sight of the clergy-man's buttocks beginning to redden, and she struck him a little more violently, "and that—and that—and that!"

She was awakening to the fact that Arthur was not so foolish after all, and she slapped away as hard as she could, hitting alternately each cheek of the bottom with her open palm, and now and then letting the tops of his thighs have a taste of her vigour. Smack followed smack till his arse was as red as a lobster shell, and he yelled out for "mercy," although desiring to be shown none. His lady laughed with delight, only slapped the harder, but he proved the strongest naturally, and bursting from her grasp, rolled off her knees on to the floor, where he lay on his back smiling ruefully up at her with his great insolent prick stiffly standing, and lolling gently from side to side by its own weight, like a scaffold pole that has come unbound.

Suddenly his smile changed to an expression of pleasure, he turned up his eyes till nothing but the whites were visible, set his teeth, gave a slight groan, and, and—well, yes,—he did!

And the milky jet flying into the air truly alarmed Miss Sinclair, and caused her to regret that so much elixir had wasted its sweetness on her Brussels carpet.

Rising slowly, he adjusted himself a little, seated himself once more by her side, and, having, nothing to say, buried his head in her soft, warm bosom, and waited, reposing in soft languor.

The amorous schoolmistress first broke the gentle silence by a question full of feminine curiosity,

"Is it so nice then to be slapped and beaten?"

"Try it, dear!" was Arthur's practical, laconic, and decisive answer.

"I should like to," responded Miss Sinclair, equal to the occasion. "But how?"

"I'll show you in a jiffy, my darling," answered the

clergyman, delighted to meet with such a luscious matron and apt pupil, and suiting the action to the word, he soon arranged the following group, which I can recommend to the attention of all "bum-bruisers" and "backside bashers," especially the partially impotent ones, whose instrument of pleasure begins to droop and get limp in the middle, betraying its master at the most critical and enchanting moment.

Arthur placed himself on his back on the sofa and directed the schoolmistress to straddle across him, her spinal column turned towards his face. She giggled, and made a few trifling objections, just as a matter of form, but she was eager to try the bastinado, and so Arthur's member, although now not as stiff as might have been desired, was soon ensconced in the clinging folds of her eager orifice.

Arthur lay like the Sultan of Turkey, or rather like the Pope, who, as the song says, "leads a happy life," and lazily moved his fatigued instrument in and out of the well-moistened crack, watching the while the contours of her immense bottom, the fully-exposed aperture above, so dear to the Jesuits, and the workings of the lips of the cunt that held him well inside.

His new conquest began to trot, then broke into a furious gallop, and he felt the warmth of a fresh libation, that galvanised him into fresh life, and reminded him that he had a task to perform, namely, that of slapping the marble bum now half covered with the chemise that had fallen over it.

This obstacle removed, the reverend rake lost no time in bringing down his right hand with just enough force to redden the part, on the right cheek of her willing backside.

This was soon followed by some slaps on the left side, and soon two red patches showed the havoc begun.

She was not hurt yet, but was only laughing as she dashed away on her charming ride, trying to spend as often as she could before her lover's crisis should come.

The consummate libertine had, however, only just commenced his part of the sport, and these preparatory blows were simply intended to deaden and benumb as much as possible the interesting hillocks that he fully meant to torture as much as he could, with a view to his own egotistical pleasure.

He was now as stiff as a ram's horn, but he let his partner do all the moving and wriggling, enchanting his eyes, and delighting his heart, as he viewed the interesting coat of varnish that his prick was gradually receiving.

He rested awhile, glancing like a connoisseur at the marks of his ten fingers, and gloating over the idea that these immaculate posteriors would soon be covered with bruises.

The thought sent a rush of blood to his head, he lifted his two hands with tremendous force, and dashed them down on her bum.

"Oh! Not so hard, dear—don't!"

Never a word did he hear, he was too much occupied in beating her with all his strength, as he furiously pushed into her cunt.

How he battered away at her unprotected bottom, heedless of all sighs, groans, and tears, as Miss Sinclair laughed and cried, groaned for mercy, then spent, and entreated him in the same breath to "stop" and "go on."

He never cared, but after a few minutes that seemed an age to his victim, drew a long breath, struck harder than ever, took a last look at the backside that he had bruised out of all knowledge, and, for the third time sent a copious jet of manly sperm into the already brimming cunt of the lascivious lady of Verbena House.

Tired, dazed, her bottom smarting with pain, and her head bursting with pleasure. She got off her champion, the effort, as she released her now drooping prisoner, causing a liquid lump of mingled male and female spendings to fall on his belly with a regular splash.

"Oh! that was lovely," she sighed, "I didn't mind how much you hurt me, Arthur, dear, the sensation was delicious." And their lips met in a tender, loving kiss.

Five minutes later all the disorder of the room has been re-arranged, the sofa is set straight once more, the pillows are beaten up, and the antimacassars replaced and smoothed out.

Seated in front of each other, separated by a round table covered with goody-goody books and photographic albums, and, tasting a peculiar old and dry sherry, a present from a pupil's wealthy father, the smug clergyman and the prim schoolmistresses are conversing as if they were saints, and not the lascivious flagellants we know them to be.

The door is unlocked and left ajar, and the subject of their talk is the projected punishment of the "young ladies" Miss Hazeltine and Miss Hatherton.

Miss Sinclair's eyes are sparkling with sherry and lust as she registers a vow to become a fearless heroine of the birch, and make the sufferings of her pupils minister to her devices.

Arthur applauds the design, whispers his evil counsel in her ear, and soon the two accomplices, equal devotees of the rod, arrange their plans for the morrow's correction, with what success the reader will see if he or she has only patience enough to read on to the end.

Having read thus far, it is well nigh certain that the gentle reader will bear with me a few pages more.

The sun struggled through the thick curtains of the schoolmistress's bedroom, searching out every chink, and managing artfully to dart a malicious ray right into the left eye of Miss Sinclair, who had enjoyed a sweet night's rest after the memorable day which she had passed in whipping Miss Bellasis, and being right royally rogered by the lascivious Arthur of the long tool.

She turned round, yawned, and found that she had been sleeping with her nightgown pushed up to her breasts, contrary to her usual habit. She smiled as she thought of what had passed, and her fingers stole to the cleft as she closed her eyes again, and reflected upon the delights of the day before.

Her principal pre-occupation was the fear of suddenly becoming enceinte.

She was so delighted at having been treated with such liberality; so pleased at the deluge of manly sperm that had lubricated her privates, that contrary to all dictates of prudence, she could not bring it over her heart to wash herself, but had passed the evening revelling in the feeling of knowing that her fat cunt was "gluey," sticky, perspiring, and strong smelling.

The beneficent shower had done her good, and made her feel a few years younger, but she resolved, with a regretful sigh, to syringe herself well out in future, in accordance with the dictates of Bradlaugh and Besant.

With this prudent resolve strong in her mind, she rose from her couch, and her first idea was to proceed to her swing-glass, where lilting up her nightgown, she peeped over her shoulder and surveyed the damage done to her fair backside.

The buttocks were dotted all over with little red spots, like pimple heads that had been well scratched, and they showed to advantage on the violet hue of the discoloured skin.

She gently scratched them and enjoyed the sensation. Then she scratched her waist, just above the hips, and, finally, her shoulder blades. Her mouth watered as she enjoyed the gentle irritation. She was a voluptuous, sensual creature, and Arthur had awakened sentiments that she had long thought were dead within her.

A hand-mirror is what she now requires, and this object—in ivory, if you please, the present of an Indian pupil—is placed between her massive thighs, while her left hand holds up her drapery.

She has a splendid view of her magnificent gap, and is pleased to see that the lips are neatly closed, and that the exertions of yesterday have not stretched it, nor caused it to gape and show the pink recesses of the interior.

She pulls it open now, and finds it caked with white flakes. Her tangled bush is also adorned with little particles of snowy wafers. She laughs to herself as she sees these traces of the storm, and curiously examines one little stalactite, holding it between her finger and thumb. This causes her to smell her fingers.

"Oh, you dirty thing!" she playfully ejaculates to herself, as she dropped her shift; and, extracting her porcelain vase from the night-table, squatted over it, and rattled out a stream like an old horse, enough to knock the bottom out of the pot.

Then she farted, first timidly, and then loudly, with a long, joyous, trumpeting sound, and at last, delivered of wind and water, she felt better, and murmured to herself:

"I wonder how Arthur's bottom looks now? I wonder, too, if it is as red as mine?"

And she rang her bell for hot water, and her bath, wishing to cleanse herself thoroughly, with a view to carry out the plan agreed upon between herself and her lover.

A loose summer toilette was soon complete, and Miss Sinclair, fresh and sweet-smelling, left her room.

She wore no drawers, and her stays were loosely laced over a neat chemise of light-blue foulard silk, trimmed with Valenciennes. A white piqué dressing gown completed all, and only showed the black silk stockings, with clocks of old gold, and her small feet encased in a pair of high-heeled shoes of glistening patent leather.

The pupils were hard at work at their morning duties. They were all very good and obedient, and the subdued buzz of their voices filled the staircase as the schoolmistress descended, and made her think that the young devils were all the better for a little old-fashioned, English correction.

She could not resist the pleasure of paying a visit to Miss Bellasis as she passed the door of the big girl's dormitory, the "Fourth Room", wishing to see the effects of her flogging, and her mind full of strange yearnings again.

She turned the knob without knocking, and walked on through the double line of neat wooden compartments. Al the girls were down stairs in the schoolroom, with the exception of the culprit, who had been allowed to remain between the sheets.

In the last cabin but one, on the side of the room where the windows were pierced in the wall, lay the proud Catherine, sleeping peacefully and soundly, in the biggest cot of the three that her "cubicle" contained.

Her eyes were still red, but a pretty flush was on her cheek, and one arm was thrown above her head, shrouded with masses of long black hair. This position had forced her two small breasts into view, and they were of a sweet golden hue, reminding one, for colour and hardness, of two Ribstone pippins.

"Poor dear!" said Miss Sinclair to herself, "no doubt she succumbed to a sudden temptation. I ought not to let one girl have more money in her possession than another. How soundly she sleeps. There is not much the matter with her now."

She touched her pupil on the shoulder, ever so lightly.

The little piece of mischief opened her eyes, and seeing her schoolmistress, flushed deeply.

"Oh! Miss Sinclair," she said, in a humble tone, proving how her proud spirit had been crushed, "I hope you have forgiven me."

"Of course I have, my dear; you have paid the penalty of your fault, and nothing more shall be said about it."

She bent down and kissed her forehead tenderly, enjoying the warmth of her healthy young skin, and inhaling the fragrance of the virgin bed.

"I will be such a good girl in future, Miss Sinclair," murmured the poor creature, her lustrous black eyes filling with tears.

"Hush, hush, Miss Catherine; don't fatigue or worry yourself," and she patted her cheek; "I'll send you up some beef tea."

There was a slight pause now, and Miss Sinclair pulled up the bedclothes and hid the girl's bosom, turning to go. Then she asked, hesitatingly:

"And tell me—hem!—how are you?"

"Oh!" said Miss Bellasis, guessing the import of the question, "Mrs. Rumble was very kind, she covered me with napkins, anointed with cold cream and potato flour, and I feel quite cool at present. I am bandaged up like a mummy all round."

Miss Sinclair was rather annoyed at the ingenious answer; she was evidently doomed never to see and admire the sexual development of her handsome pupil.

With a few more kind words she left her victim, and went about her usual duties, registering a mental vow that Miss Hazeltine and Miss Hatherton should not baulk her salacious wishes that afternoon, for the flogging was to take place in private.

Her excuse should be that she did not wish to demoralise her pupils by such continual public castigations; which, to tell the truth, were a little bit repulsive and disgusting.

But her true thoughts were that nothing was so entrancing and so provocative of sensual enjoyment, and that with doors closed, and no under-governesses to spy upon her, she could tickle the wretched girls' blushing backsides to her heart's content. She could flog slowly or quickly, and she could turn and twist them about to her liking, varying the postures as she fancied. She dreamt of other instruments besides the ordinary bundle of rods, and cogitated deeply on the idea of striking the loins only, for a change.

"I must ask Arthur," she murmured to herself, "he must tell me all about that hair-brush execution he mentioned. I should like to do that to him, but he must be tied down, so that I could revel at the idea of having the strong fellow in my power. I would not hurt him much though. I would only make his dear bottom all red and nice! Yes; that would be lovely."

The time had slipped away so rapidly that our lady flagellant had forgotten to order a fresh supply of birch, so she determined to use other implements, especially as the punishment was to take place in private. It was better that the neighbouring shop-keepers should not know that so many rods were now wanted at Verbena House.

The breakfast was over, and towards noon a discreet ring at the bell marked "visitors," announced the Reverend Arthur, who, as neat as usual, but a little flushed, walked into the hall, as the door was opened by Mrs. Rumble.

She winked in a vulgar manner, that Arthur tried not to see, and said:

"All right, Sir, I've got to take you upstairs to the Red Room. Missus will be soon ready to see you."

The gentleman was too "thick in the mouth" to answer, but as he put his umbrella in the rack, and hung up his hat, he felt in his waistcoat pocket and then slipped a half-crown piece into the house-keeper's willing hand.

"Thank you, kindly, Sir," she said with a curtsey, "there's two of 'em going to be 'done over' today."

"Yes, yes; I know!" he answered impatiently, and Mrs. Rumble led him quietly to the top of the house, taking care that no one should see him, or, indeed, know of his presence in the school.

No sooner was he left alone in the little red-baized apartment, Mrs. Rumble having gone down to apprise her mistress of his expected arrival, than he drew a long breath, and took a steady look all around him.

"So this is the place where the two minxes are going to be polished off, is it?" he soliloquised. "Where shall I be able to conceal myself? Here, in this bedroom adjoining. The door can be closed, but I shall have a front row at the pretty theatre of castigation."

And, drawing a gimlet from his pocket, he quickly pierced a big hole in the corner of one of the panels of the door, blew away the sawdust, applied his eye, and tried how much he could see.

He had a full view in front of the door.

In the corner of the so-called Red Room stood a large, clumsy, old-fashioned easel, and on it was a black board of portentous size. He drew this off and dragged the upright apparatus right into the middle of the chamber, directly facing his peep hole. Then he picked up the black board, carried it to the wall, and stood it up on end, right behind the easel, in a direct line with it.

"Their flesh will show better against the black, and I shall have a fine view in my little snuggery."

Footsteps were now heard upon the stairs, so drawing hastily four new straps, fitted with buckles, from his pockets, he laid them upon the easel, and darting into the bedroom, closed the door after him.

He was no sooner landed in his retreat, and his eye applied to the orifice made by the gimlet, than the door of the Red Room suddenly opened, and one of the young ladies was propelled violently into the middle of the apartment, where she stood with her handkerchief to her eyes, bellowing right loudly, and evidently in an agony of fright.

Miss Sinclair's voice could be heard outside as she stood upon the landing, telling Mrs. Rumble and Miss Cope that "she did not need their assistance, and preferred to punish the wicked bad girl alone."

She entered the room, carrying a small parcel wrapped up in a pocket handkerchief, which she placed on the ledge of the easel, after carefully bolting the door. Her eye lighted on the straps, she smiled to herself, looked towards the panelling that artful Arthur had just pierced, licked her hot lips with a gormandizing expression of countenance, and called out loudly, as she frowned, and pretended to be in a dreadful passion.

"Miss Haseltine!"

This young person left off howling, put down her well-wetted square of cambric, and showed a tearful face, that surmounted a slight, well-made frame, shaken by convulsive sobs.

She was a growing girl of about fourteen, pale and thin, with large eyes, and a quantity of fair hair, of no particular colour at all just at present.

A doctor would soon have guessed from the diaphanous quality of her skin that she was inclined to be poor-blooded, and if not treated with great care at the epoch of her change from girlhood to the womanly state, would very likely be all her life a martyr to amenia and the "whites". But she was pretty, nevertheless, and her pallor made her look interesting and pre-Raphaelitisch—something like an early Christian martyr.

Miss Sinclair could see that her slender body was not capable of receiving very much punishment, so she resolved to tease her well, and prolong the scene of lecture, humiliation and correction, for the benefit of her lusty lover, whose hand was already on his partially-standing staff of life. He had got on an old pair of "bags," with the right hand pocket cut out—a method which I recommend either to habitual masturbators, or to any one who is going out with his "light o' love."

On a long journey, or even during a promenade of any kind, the lady's white and soft palm is always acceptable, if only to show her the effect her bright eyes have created. A gentle rubbing of the testicles will pass away the time without producing emission, and there is less danger of surprise by railway porters, coachmen, servants, and other necessary spies of society.

She need not even take off her glove, but the top of the penis can be inserted under the warm kid, or soft

Suède leather, and a fair imitation of the inimitable female "pussy" is thus produced.

It has been my lot to travel the wide world over on special missions, and I have sometimes been very much afraid of chance strokes by rail, steamers, or even lumbering old deligences. To this plan I have, therefore, resorted when circumstances, modesty on the part of the angel, or lack of cash on mine, has prevented me having a mellow, luscious, sweet, gamahuche, blistering pederastie encounter, or ejaculation between the breasts, in the fashion yclept "bag-piping."

"Miss Haseltine!" reiterated the schoolmistress, "what was in that bottle?"

"Gin, Ma'am!" and the silly thing thought it her duty to start whimpering and crying again.

"And why do you drink gin, if you please?" continued her tormentor, hardly able to keep from smiling.

"Oh! if you please, I would much rather not tell. Boo—hoo! And I won't be whipped! And I'll tell my father. Oh! I'm so miserable."

"You little cat," said Miss Sinclair, "I'll take all your naughtiness out of you."

And, going to the easel, she opened the parcel, which contained a hair-brush, a riding whip, a bottle of arnica, and a book.

Armed with the lithe switch, she marched upon the cowering, weeping girl and gave her a smart cut over the fleshy part of her arms, one blow on each shoulder.

Miss Haseltine roared dismally, and dropped to her knees, rubbing the inflamed parts with a piteous air.

"Now will you tell me?"

"You are so cruel!" she whimpered, sniffing up her sobs, "but, if you must know, the other big girls said that I should not be a woman if I did not have what some of them have got every month, and—and—they said that drinking gin would bring on the nasty things, so I got some, and I didn't drink much, because it made me feel so funny. And, oh! Miss Sinclair, don't beat me, and I'll never drink any more."

"You bad character; I'll soon prevent your thoughts running upon such unchaste, unmaidenly topics. Strip!"

And a whistling cut through the air accentuated this dire command.

The poor girl saw it was useless to contend any longer against the stern resolves of her schoolmistress, so she rose up and began slowly to disrobe. Getting out of her dress and crinoline, she stood blushing, trembling, and crying in her shift, stays, and long ridiculous drawers, which were plain, split up, baggy, and decorated with "tucks," to let out for "growing."

"Go on," said Miss Sinclair, enjoying her confusion, and the sight of two red marks on either arm, making her gloating eyes flash fire.

"Oh! please, Madam; do let me off this time," she pleaded, slowly undoing her stays.

"I'll let you off, by and by, never fear."

And Miss Haseltine burst into a fresh fit of weeping, as the tiny corset dropped to the ground. Miss Sinclair advanced, and undid the drawers herself, shook her out of them roughly, and dragged the chemise right over her head.

The maiden was naked with the exception of stockings and boots. She looked very pretty indeed, but a trifle too thin. Her ribs could be counted, but she possessed small, pear-shaped breasts, that were surprisingly hard and stiff, with neatly-defined, light-pink nipples. Her poor little dickey-bird was only just beginning to be fledged with down, of the curly chestnut pattern.

Her executioner literally revelled in the coy shame of the young woman who stood stark naked, first trying to hide her bosom, and then placing one hand over the little dented mark that had never experienced the attack of manly vigour.

In spite of her spasmodic weeping, cries and entreaties, Miss Sinclair dragged her to the easel, and, forcing her arms above her head, fastened with the straps each wrist to the uprights right and left. Stooping next she dragged the legs apart, and with the remaining bonds buckled them to the lower supports, thus "spread-eagling" the unfortunate Miss Haseltine.

She stepped back and admired her work, looked towards the bed-room, and laughed, as she guessed Arthur could see her.

Then she set her teeth, pulled up the right sleeve of her dressing gown, and directed a terrific blow at the loins of her victim, drawing forth a long shriek of agony.

A long red line could now be seen across the small of the back, just above a little, smooth, white bottom, like a boy's.

Another blow, now on the left cheek, also elicited a faint cry from the damsel; and then the right buttock came in for a flicking cut with the whip-cord at the end, drawing at once a small spot of blood.

Miss Sinclair could see that her skin was remarkably fine and tender and would take but little chastisement. Besides, the girl was fluttering all over, like a caged bird, and her gasps for breath were painfully loud, while her sobs seemed almost to choke her.

So Miss Sinclair braced herself up for the final touch and rained down a reckless shower of blows, that the bound up beauty in vain tried to avoid by stretching, and wriggling about.

She only succeeded in affording a magnificent view of her little distended orifice to Miss Sinclair and consequently to Arthur. At the same time, in the middle of her distended posteriors, could be seen her small brown anus, that throbbed and wrinkled up distinctly.

Her tiny quim, with its pale-coral lining, made the mistress of Verbena House feel like a fury, and she flogged away again, unheeding the cries of the martyred pupil, which were positively appalling.

I will not swear that one or two blows did not seek out and tingle the pretty part that Miss Bellasis had disappointed her tormentor by never showing at all.

Although this girl had not received half as much punishment as her comrade Kate the day before, her bum presented a much worse appearance, as the whip had cut into the skin, which was much finer and thinner in texture.

The blood had flown at once and in quantities forcing Miss Sinclair to drop her weapon, and having recourse to the tincture of arnica, she rubbed it into the cuts, giving fresh pain, but stopping the blood, and preventing subsequent discolouring.

Miss Haseltine had had enough, and could only give vent to deep groans, as Miss Sinclair undid the straps, and assisted her to dress, petting and soothing her, and assuring her that the "slight correction" was only for her good.

The girl was too cowed and distressed to utter a word, besides, the tincture was so smarting to her rump, that it made her tearful eyes blink again, as her tormentor dismissed her to bed, telling her at the same time to let Miss Cope know that her playmate, Miss Hatherton, was wanted "for punishment" in a few minutes.

No sooner was the girl gone than Miss Sinclair bolted the door after her, and, turning round, was caught in the arms of the reverend lecher, who emerged from his retirement, with his fiery pendulum protruding boldly from his open breeches.

"I must have you now, darling," he exclaimed, his voice thick with lustful excitement, and a colourless, pearly drop starting from the urethra.

"No! no! not now, Arthur!," protested his mistress, struggling to release herself, while she returned his kisses all the same, thrusting her thirsty tongue between his willing lips, "I can't with my stays on."

"I must come, anyhow," cried the clergyman, who was perfectly reckless with desire, and, thrusting her to her knees, he rubbed the top of his weapon against her lips, evidently trying to force it into her mouth.

I am forced to confess that at that moment Miss Sinclair was evidently not sufficiently expert in love's diversions to care about the amiable favour that was demanded of her.

Was she too shy? or did she only desire to keep Arthur's emission for more enjoyable copulation later on? It is impossible to say, as I never could fathom the mysteries of the female mind, but nevertheless her conqueror was determined not to be put off.

He rapidly unfastened the buttons of her loose wrapper, slipping it over her shoulders, and dragging her arms out of the sleeves with scant ceremony, he soon had her neck and shoulders exposed to view.

Getting behind her, despite her remonstrances, he held her on her knees with one hand, and with the other placed his rubicund affair under her armpit, forcing her to hold her arm tight to her side.

A few short drives among the thick undergrowth, and against the warm, perspiring, soft flesh, soon brought the requisite effect into play, the tickling of the hair greatly aiding and producing divine satisfaction.

The first spurt of joy sent a shower of spray right across the room, and the rest slowly dripped down on to the warm bosom of the lady, who was very excited, never having taken eyes off the top of her favourite, as it appeared once or twice in front of her arm.

"You naughty boy!" she exclaimed, as Arthur now let her rise from her kneeling posture, "I'll whip you for this;" and she re-adjusted her dress, wiping away the remains of the copious libation with a lace handkerchief.

Arthur replied with a kiss, and Miss Sinclair smote lightly the principal offender, who hung his diminished head, while "a tear fell gently from his eye."

There was a timid knock now at the door of the bedroom, and Miss Sinclair, placing her finger on her lip, made the reverend gentleman retreat, and opening the door directly he was under cover, gave entrance to Miss Hatherton, who stood in the doorway with a hesitating expression of countenance, and her under-lip quivering with suppressed emotion.

"Come in; bad girl! You are the last I have to chastise, and I hope this will be the end of all wickedness in my flock!" and she bolted the door.

This sounded very well, but it was far from sincere, and made Arthur chuckle to himself in his hiding place.

"I won't allow you to touch me, and if you do the Archdeacon shall know by the very next post."

"Indeed!" said Miss Sinclair, slowly, "I pray you listen to me. Your father distinctly told me that I was to correct you whenever I chose, and in whatever manner I thought fit. It appears your vile instincts have manifested themselves at home before, and I can show you a line or two from your respected father, to whom you alluded just now, where he mentions a little contretemps that occurred last winter, while the church was being decorated for Christmas, and all the young people were together."

This unexpected revelation struck Miss Hatherton dumb, and two large tears issuing slowly from her eyes coursed gently down her cheeks.

She was a stout girl, and one of the kind that would blossom into the traditional "fine woman," all arse and bubbies. Her complexion was florid, and she had fine white teeth. The picture of health, in fact; the type of a fair brunette with a fair skin, like the beauties of Ireland.

Miss Sinclair took up the book which was plainly bound, and bore stamped upon the back these two letters—"F. H."

"What is this volume, if you please?" said Miss Sinclair, holding it a long way from her, between her finger and thumb, as if it was about to go off.

Miss Hatherton did not answer; so Miss Sinclair stamped her foot and advanced a step, the girl putting up her hand as if to ward off a blow.

"Fanny Hill!" suddenly answered the culprit.

"Fanny who?"

"Fanny Hill! A bad woman."

Miss Sinclair opened the pages, and pretending to see the coloured lithographs it contained for the first time, dropped it in feigned disgust, and shrieked out:

"You nasty vicious, horrid wretch of a girl, whatever will become of you? Where did you get it from?"

"I found it at the baths, the last time we went;" was the slow answer she gave.

"I don't believe you," rejoined the schoolmistress, "you are a liar, as well as a—a—," and she stopped short for an epithet, not knowing any more than I should how to qualify a young lady who reads

Cleland's delightful novel at the age of sixteen-and-a-half.

"Oblige me by taking off your dress," Miss Sinclair continued, "and should you prove obedient, and submit to your punishment meekly, promising never to offend again, I promise not to cause more pain than is absolutely needful to drive all bad thoughts out of you."

Miss Hatherton was crying silently, but, deluded by the half-promise of Miss Sinclair, she gave up any idea of revolt that might have germed in her mind, and, undoing her dress, stood before the schoolmistress in her stays, chemise, stockings, and boots, but with no drawers on.

"What!" exclaimed Miss Sinclair, "why is this?"

"Have got too stout for mine, which are tight ones, and button at the side."

"You slovenly, dirty thing."

And Miss Sinclair pulled up her shift, which was ridiculously short, the poor thing having evidently grown out of all her under-linen.

Truth compels me to confess what Miss Sinclair, and Arthur staring through his gimlet-hole, could easily see the Archdeacon's daughter was a martyr to self-abuse. She was already, thanks to her precocious practices, developed like a woman, with plenty of curly, black hair shading her parts and growing on her belly.

The lips of her quim were slightly apart, a pouting clitoris could be easily seen, and all was too red and chafed for a young boarding-school Miss.

"Your habits are vile," said Miss Sinclair, "and I think that I shall not correct you at all, but simply send you home to night."

"Don't do that!" cried the girl, in an agony of terror. "Beat me; kill me, if you like; but don't send me away from your school. I will repent, and never touch myself again, I promise you. I can't help it. All the girls do it at Saltcross Marsh, they do, indeed."

Showers of tears choked all further utterances, as Miss Sinclair led her to the improvised "horse," and attached her hands to the uprights, exactly as she had done to her predecessor.

Taking up the hairbrush, she said to her powerless pupil:

"I hope what you are going to suffer will do you some real good, and cure you of your awful propensities. I shall put you under the care of Dr. Jossop to-morrow, and should I find an amendment a little while, I will keep your shameful secret, and your father shall not know what a bad daughter he has."

Of course she did not want to send her away. The Archdeacon never disputed a single item of the bill, and there were lots of "sundries" and "extras" that could always be tacked on to the big girls' accounts.

"Thank you, Miss Sinclair. I will try and merit your good opinion in future. But oh! do make haste, and get it over," she could not help adding, betraying the agonizing suspense of her feelings.

Miss Sinclair tucked her chemise under her stays, and disclosed to the eyes of the randy watcher a fine fat bottom, almost matured. She was fixed up rather high, so that her toes just touched the floor, and the strained attitude caused her to throw back her shoulders, as she tried to see what Miss Sinclair was doing, and arch out her posterior.

Her schoolmistress, who was trembling with anticipatory delight, took up the hairbrush. It was not an ordinary flat-bristled one, but the long hairs being placed in the middle of the wood, and shorter kinds all round, formed a rounded top of fine points, making what Truefitt and Hopgood, the two principal hairdressers of London-super-Mare, called "The Flexible."

This was not to be a delicate, scientific, long drawn-out flagellation, as Miss Sinclair was a deal too excited to go gently to work. The effects of the first flogging combined with Arthur's attack, had driven her to the verge of desperation, and the wretched victim peering round was horrified at the determined look on her schoolmistress's face.

Miss Sinclair was livid, as she clutched the formidable brush, and her eyes glared, while her clenched teeth shone out white and terrible.

Miss Hatherton made a pitiful appeal for mercy, which only excited the cruel woman more, and burst into a shower of tears, that was the signal for instant execution.

The bristles descended with a brutal thump right in the middle of the left buttock, raising at once a round red mark, with the multitude of points imprinted on the skin. With devilish ingenuity the companion posterior came in for just such another blow, so that the bottom was well decorated on either posterior.

Miss Sinclair was too busily engaged in enjoying the fun to lecture the girl, or, indeed, speak at all. She let Miss Hatherton howl, beg for pity, and blurt out wild promises for amendment, without paying the least attention, as she stepped back to enjoy the pleasurable sight of the ill-treated backside, and also to afford a clear view to her hidden accomplice.

As she approached again, the weapon uplifted, Miss Hatherton, in great fright, kicked out and writhed about as if she could by so doing avert the coming blow. Her tormentor laughed scornfully at the useless effort, and taking up one of the remaining straps, she fastened her left leg only to the corresponding support of the easel, and, holding the right leg herself very tightly, disclosed by a smart pull the whole of Miss Hatherton's open cunt.

It was an easy task to do so, as the big lips had been often played with and distended by the fair disciple of Onan, and very little of the hymen was apparently left. The red, staring orifice was far from being pretty to look at, and it is possible that a feeling of disgust on the part of Miss Sinclair caused her to ply her brush very freely.

It was dashed down all over the bottom and top of the thighs with a regular bump—bump—bump; each time being pressed down as the stroke was delivered, so as to leave a new impression of all the cutting ends of the bristles.

The tortured bottom was all over a fiery crimson, and soon the little holes made in the skin distilled small drips of blood, as if a million of pins had pricked the flesh.

The cries of the girl grew fainter and fainter as her strength to bear the excessive pain diminished. She no longer wriggled about, depriving Miss Sinclair thereby of the delight her struggles had afforded, as she held her leg in her grasp.

The schoolmistress reserved her hand for a final effort, and her heart beating as if it would burst her stays, lifted the brush and cruelly assaulted the inside of Miss Hatherton's robust thigh, turning "The Flexible" round, so as to attack each side of the polished column in turn.

They were soon as red and bruised as the rest, and Miss Sinclair stopped to take breath. Miss Hatherton broke into a fresh fit of hysterical weeping, mingled with choking sobs and deep moans of pain.

The communicating door was now carefully held ajar, and Arthur's face, his eyes lit up with a demon glare of cruelty and lust, was seen peering through, as he whispered:

"Miss Sinclair!"

She turned round, started, and signed to him to go back.

He pointed to Miss Hatherton, and motioning with his left hand, for his right held his slimy-standing prick, performed the gesture of striking vertically upwards, while he murmured but this one word, in a deep, solemn, eager whisper:

"Up!"

Miss Sinclair understood but to well, and raising the brush, she poised it between the archway formed by the outstretched thighs, the bristles just touching the delicate parts, and pulling the leg she held towards her, flicked the brush right into the gaping quim.

The pain must have been awful, as the girl's whole frame quivered with agony, and giving a long shriek, her head dropped on her shoulder, her eyes closed, an ashy paleness overspread her countenance, and she fainted away, leaving Arthur and Miss Sinclair to gloat over the spectacle of her bruised bum, and distended, inflamed cunt, which had become a deep magenta colour, tinged with blue, from the effects of the rousing "cut up."

* * * * *

Having shown our readers how Miss Bellasis was "Birched for Thieving," and how the Mistress of Verbena House became a flagellant, our task is done.

Not a girl in the school went home for the holidays without having been "corrected" in some way or another, and the Reverend Arthur was always to the fore, his manly powers being strengthened by the ever-changing spectacles provided by his sensual mistress. He touted for pupils among the mothers who devoutly "sat under him," and soon Verbena House became one of the best schools in Brighton, turning out the most obedient accomplished ladies possible, and transforming dirty, slovenly, lazy, dunces into stately maidens, who excited the admiration of all beholders as they filed down the Marine Parade, two by two, with smiling faces, albeit aching bottoms.

It was Stiggles who betrayed to me the secrets I have disclosed in the foregoing narrative. It was he who got the gin for Miss Haseltine, the book for Miss Hatherton, and he concluded his boyish career by raising Dolly's belly. This last exploit got him the sack. He became "boots" to the Ship Hotel. There I met him, and his discovery of one of the late Mr. Dugdale's works in my travelling bag, caused him to wax confidential, and tell me what I have tried to describe.

My only hope is that those flagellants who peruse my work may become more ardent in their pursuit of bottoms to whack than ever, and that those who have never tickled a male or female arse, may commence at once.

Above all, let the weaker sex have a sight at these pages, for while female flagellants exist, England will never want for soldiers or sailors, or bright-eyed obedient, sensible housewives.

FINIS

BIRCHGROVE PRESS

Flagellant & Libertine Erotica

Birchgrove Press specializes in producing new print and e-book editions of pre-1950s writings on sexual flagellation in English. Original editions of many of the books that we offer are difficult to obtain and are highly sought after. We are especially proud to offer new editions of rare Victorian flagellant texts such as *The Mysteries of Verbena House*, *Experimental Lecture by Colonel Spanker*, and *The Quintessence of Birch Discipline*. Birchgrove Press also produces new editions of libertine literature. We have published *Venus in the Cloister*, *The School of Venus*, *The Dialogues of Luisa Sigea*, and Isidore Liseux's translation of the Marquis de Sade's *Justine* (1791), *Opus Sadicum*, for example.

www.birchgrovepress.com.